My friend Percy and Buffalo Bill

My friend
Percy
and Buffalo Bill

Ulf Stark

GECKO PRESS

Also by Ulf Stark
Can You Whistle, Johanna? (GECKO PRESS, 2005)
My Friend Percy's Magical Gym Shoes (GECKO PRESS, 2005)
My Friend Percy and the Sheik (GECKO PRESS, 2006)

© Ulf Stark 2004
First published in Sweden by Bonnier Carlsen Bokförlaget, Stockholm, Sweden
Published in the English language by arrangement with
Bonnier Carlsen Bokförlaget
Original title: *Min vän Percy, Buffalo Bill och jag*

Gecko Press gratefully acknowledges the assistance of Svenska Institutet (SI).

This edition first published in Australia and New Zealand in 2008 by
Gecko Press, PO Box 9335, Marion Square, Wellington 6141, New Zealand
Email: info@geckopress.com
English translation © Julia Marshall 2008
Edited by Raymond Huber

National Library of New Zealand Cataloguing-in-Publication Data
Stark, Ulf, 1944 –
Min vän Percy, Buffalo Bill och jag. English
My friend Percy and Buffalo Bill / by Ulf Stark.
ISBN 978-0-9582787-1-3
[1. Friendship—Fiction. 2. Vacations—Fiction.] I. Stark, Ulf,
1944- Min vän Percy, Buffalo Bill och jag. II. Title.
839.738—dc 22

Cover design: Sarah Maxey, Nice Work
Typesetting: Archetype
Printing: Everbest, China

ISBN: 978-0-9582787-1-3

For more curiously good books, visit
www.geckopress.com

Contents

I become a blood brother

You look forward to some days more than others.

We'd been waiting for this one for almost a year. The sun was shining through the classroom window. It spread a cheerful light on our brushed-and-combed heads and on the red apple Anna-Christine had put on the teacher's desk. We'd cleaned out our desks and life was looking pretty good.

We were breaking up for the summer holidays.

I was thinking about Klaus, and Pia, and the smell of nettles. I was thinking about my fat, angry grandfather, and how good it would be to dive into the bubbling waves behind the boats in the archipelago.

Then my friend Percy tapped me on the shoulder and passed me a crinkled piece of paper. It said,

WE'LL LEAVE AS SOON AS THEY START SINGING!

The teacher went up to the piano.

"Now then," she said. "Let's have a song."

She was a relief teacher. Her lips were painted red, she had red shoes, and she wore a thin red belt made from genuine plastic. When she moved, her yellow dress rippled like a field of wheat in the breeze. She smelled like lily of the valley. She smiled at the parents, and they all smiled back. Her smile was infectious.

"I hope you'll all sing along," she smiled.

She played, *When the field of wheat moves in the breeze*, because that was the most beautiful song she knew. I only moved my lips so I wouldn't disturb the music. Most of the others did too. But not my mother. She warbled the high notes at the top of her voice, like she always did.

I winked to Percy that it was time to go. I knew Mum wouldn't like it. But what was she making a noise like that for?

We stood up and walked out of the classroom. Percy took the apple from the teacher's desk on his way out. We ran through the corridors. When we got to the school gate, we were met by blinding sun, chirping birds and a sky that went on forever.

"Cripes," I thought.

We raced to the jump tower where, in winter, the ski-jumpers would line up waiting for their turn to race down the hill. We sat at the top. A warm wind was blowing in the tree tops, ruffling our best haircuts. We stuck our school ties in our trouser pockets and took off our shoes and socks, so our toes could start their summer holidays too.

Percy divided the apple as evenly as he could with his pocket knife and then he took the biggest bit.

"What're you doing for summer?" he asked.

"I'm going to the island," I said. "We go there every year."

"What do you do there?"

"Heaps of things. What are you doing for summer?"

Percy didn't answer. He frowned, spat some apple pips out and looked over towards the slaughterhouse. He seemed almost worried for a moment. Then he tested the edge of his knife with his thumb and his eyes lit up.

"We've known each other a long time now, wouldn't you say?"

"That's right," I said.

"How long, do you think?"

"Three years."

"That's right," he said. "That means it's time for us to become blood brothers."

"Blood brothers? What's that?" I asked.

"It's when you each cut your finger and you mix blood," explained Percy. "What a piece of luck I brought my knife with me."

He wiped the dirty blade on his trouser leg. I suddenly remembered all the times I'd had blood tests.

"Good idea," I said. "But it might get infected. If you get blood poisoning you can die, you know."

My father was a dentist, so I knew quite a lot about bacteria.

"True," said Percy. "But not if you heat the blade up first."

I couldn't think of anything else to say. Percy always carried a box of matches. He lit one and held the edge of the blade over the flame till it was black with soot. Then he made a small cut, first in his own thumb, and then in mine. It hurt. But it also felt good in a funny kind of way, as if it was a special occasion.

"There," he said. "Now we're blood brothers. Do you know what that means?"

"No," I said.

"It means that you each go with the other one when he goes to an island," said Percy. "But I don't have an island to go to. So I'll have to come with you to yours."

I wasn't sure I wanted him to. It's true that Percy was my best friend. But I had a lot of other friends on the island. There was Klaus and Benke, Ulf E and Leif. And there was Pia. I wondered if Percy would get on with them. And Mum and Dad might not think it was a good idea to bring Percy. My brother definitely wouldn't.

And I was dead sure Grandpa wouldn't want any more children in the house.

My brother and I were already two too many.

Grandpa didn't like children.

He didn't like grown-ups or animals either.

"I don't know," I said. "Grandpa is always so incredibly angry."

"Doesn't matter – I'm not scared," said Percy. "I've never been to an island."

"Promise you won't annoy him then?" I said.

"You know me."

I did. That's what worried me. If there was anyone who could annoy anybody, it was Percy. But I couldn't say no to my freshly-cut blood brother.

"You'll have to come a bit later," I said. "Give me a chance to sort it out."

"When shall I come?"

"Twelfth of July. That's my birthday," I said.

Percy hugged me so hard we rolled down the hill.

"Happy birthday in advance!" he said.

When I got home I could smell burnt pork right through the house.

Mum was upset.

"How could you run off like that before the class break up was even finished?" she said. "How could you be so stupid? Now I've gone and burnt the dinner. What came over you, Ulf?"

"I needed to pee," I said.

"And Percy?"

"He did too," I said.

I had picked a briar rose from Mrs Ohlson's hedge on the way home, because I knew Mum would be cross. I held it out to her and smiled my most charming smile.

"This is for you, Mother," I said.

"Thank you," she said. "But you should know that what you did wasn't a well brought-up thing to do. You must remember that your father is a dentist."

"Oops, I forgot," I said.

I bowed my head as if I was sorry. It was a good idea when Mum was upset.

"And you've got flecks of blood on those new corduroy trousers," sighed my mother, though her voice was already sounding calmer.

"I cut myself on a thorn when I was picking the rose," I said.

"Never mind," she said. "I have a washing machine. Sometimes I wonder if it's appropriate for you to spend so much time with that Percy. He's very sweet of course, deep down inside, but he gets up to so much mischief.

It's a good thing we're going to the island, so you two can be apart for a bit. What do you think?"

"Mmm, it's probably a good idea," I said.

"Then we won't say anything to your father about the break up," she said.

"No-oo," I said.

And I didn't say anything about inviting Percy to the island either.

Which is why Dad was in such a good mood at dinner. He was pleased that it was soon time to visit Grandma and Grandpa. It meant leaving his worries behind. He took a mouthful of fried cabbage, and didn't even notice that the pork was completely burnt. He smiled at my brother – who took it as an invitation to flick some dried snot onto my plate.

Dad made a joke.

"Won't it be fantastic to have peace and quiet and a view of a cow," he said.

No one laughed.

CHAPTER TWO

I fall into the water with my clothes on

I didn't get the chance before we left to tell Mum and Dad that I'd invited Percy to the island. We had so much packing to do.

I packed a drawing pad, the piece of cheese left in the fridge, and the pocket knife Grandpa had given me. My brother Jan put a stack of *Phantom* and *Steelman* comics in his bag. Mum packed two suitcases and a trunk. Dad filled his pipe.

"We're ready to go," he said.

We travelled in our boat, called *Pretto*. It was a motorboat with two masts, so you could put a sail up if the motor stopped out at sea. Mostly I stayed in the little room called a stern cabin right up the back. I ate my cheese and then I pressed my face against the floorboards till my whole head shook. That was how I made myself forget that I was seasick.

And then I thought about Pia for the same reason.

I took out my drawing pad and wrote PIA in big letters at the top of the page. I felt better already. But what did she look like? I remembered she had dark hair and a nice figure. But what did her lips look like? And her nose and eyes? How can you like someone when you can't even remember what they look like?

I drew a face with no nose, eyes or mouth. But the chin still felt wrong. Then I drew in an eye and rubbed it out again. Even the eyebrows weren't right.

"Bum," I said, so quietly that even I couldn't hear it.

Then I tried to recall her laugh. That was easier. It was a hoarse laugh that made me feel ticklish. It did last summer anyhow. I wondered if it would still sound the same.

Just then Jan pulled up the hatch and jumped down right onto my noseless, mouthless drawing.

"Nice," he said.

"Don't you ever knock?"

"Oooh, sorry, sorry, beg your pardon," he said.

He took a *Phantom* comic from his bag and hopped back out into the sun.

After a while I went out too. I folded my drawing into an aeroplane and threw it into the wind. First it circled, then it skydived, and bounced up and down on the waves, like a seagull making an emergency landing.

Dad stood at the wheel, whistling. He was wearing his white boat cap a little crooked because he was so happy. He was always happy on the way to the island. He whistled, *Now I am broke and free as a bird*, smoking his pipe at the same time. The notes blew away like small clouds. He nodded at passing islands and flocks of birds.

Mum sat in the back, knitting a jersey. I looked at a comic and tried not to think about my stomach. Even though Dad hated comics, he said nothing to me because we were on our way to the island.

"Look out starboard, Ulf, and tell me what you see," said Dad.

I looked out the wrong side. I saw seagulls diving towards a jetty and an old man coming out of the toilets.

"I don't know," I said.

"Can't you learn the difference between starboard and port?" said Dad. "I suppose it will come in time."

"I s'pose it will," I said.

He'd wanted me to see the lighthouse. Every year when we passed the lighthouse it was time to eat, because that meant we were exactly half way. Mum unpacked the picnic basket – milk, sandwiches, luncheon sausage and pickled gherkins.

"Isn't this wonderful?" Dad said.

He let go the steering wheel long enough to stroke my mother's cheek and get himself a sandwich.

"What is?" asked my mother.

"Everything," he said.

He meant being away from his dentist work and the dental nurse who always turned the taps off so tightly that the washers broke.

He meant having peace in his soul.

"Can't you sing something?" suggested Dad.

"Not while we're eating," said Mum.

But she smiled anyway. I thought this might be the right time to bring up Percy's visit.

"You know, there's something I need to tell you," I said.

"Is it something nice?" asked Mum.

"Yes, it is."

"What is it then?" asked Dad.

Jan raised his eyes from *The Secret of Skull Cave*.

"He just wants to say that he loves Pia and wants to marry her!" he said. "In the cathedral!"

"You're such a big dork," I shouted and splashed my milk in his face.

If we'd been back home Dad would have got really angry. But we were on our way to the island, so he just caught hold of Jan who was on his way to hit me, his hair dripping with milk.

"Don't tease him, Jan," said Dad. "Feelings are sensitive things. And Ulf, you shouldn't swear," he said, turning to me. "You'd better brush your teeth twice this evening. Stop fighting, children. Would you like more milk?"

I didn't. I felt sick enough already.

"Now Ulf, what was it you wanted to say?" asked Mum.

"Nothing in particular," I said and then turned to Dad. "Why do you always have to drive so pathetically slowly?"

Dad never drove faster than seven knots. He believed in having time to enjoy the view, and it also meant we used less fuel. I crept back to the cabin and put my face against the floorboards.

I came out again when Dad tooted three long signals and one short. That meant we were almost there. Grandpa and Grandma's house was right on the top of the hill, like a giant white meringue. Grandpa had built it himself. It had two towers, a flat roof and a balcony where Grandma was standing, waving a duster. Grandpa was in the garden digging up stones. He waved hello with his spade when we puttered past.

He'd raised the flag in honour of our arrival.

"Now the heavenly peace begins," said Dad when we came in to the main jetty and Jan had put down the anchor.

"Don't be too sure about that," said Mum.

"Well, I'm not planning on taking it easy anyway," I said.

12

It didn't seem as if nature was going to either. A cloud of seagulls and terns screeched above our heads. Pia was cleaning a pike over on the nearby peninsula that stuck out on the other side of the bay.

"There's your darling," said Jan, pinching me in the thigh, where no one could see him do it.

"I don't care about her," I shot back.

But I couldn't help quickly looking at her lips, eyes, nose and chin and her red bathing suit. Of course, that's what she looked like. Her body was just as nice as I remembered, except it had grown a bit since last time. Now she held up the pike and waved it.

"Hello Ulf," she called. "Will you come to the pier for a swim soon?"

"I don't think so. I'm meeting Klaus today," I answered, because my brother was standing beside me listening.

"Okay," she said, lowering the pike.

Dad had just got the trunk up on deck.

"That's a mighty big fish you have there, Pia," he puffed.

"It's nothing – my second or third bite. I got it by the other jetty," she said, and carried on cleaning the inside of the fish.

Together, Dad, Jan and I managed to get the trunk all the way to the jetty.

"I'll go and get the trolley," said Dad. "Carry on unloading."

Grandpa had put the trolley beside the alder trees near the pump, so we wouldn't have to go up to the house to get it.

When I was crossing the deck with a load of gumboots, umbrellas and raincoats in my arms, I suddenly thought of Pia's laugh. I wondered if her laugh would sound the same again this year. Then my feet decided to trip on a piece of rope. I dropped my load, waved my arms wildly and fell into the water with a splash.

It was warmer than I thought it would be.

When I came to the surface I could hear her laugh. It got mixed up with the cries of the seagulls. It was as hoarse and wild and bold as before.

"Talk about clumsy," giggled my brother.

I said nothing. I was so happy I just smiled, coughed and spouted water.

"What was that?" called Dad from behind the alders.

"It was just Ulf throwing the raincoats into the sea," called Jan.

"Give me strength," said Dad.

CHAPTER THREE

I meet Grandpa, some caterpillars and Klaus

Dad was puffing with the loaded trolley. The trunk was at the bottom. It looked like a treasure chest made from aluminium with black bands around it. It was full of clothes and sheets, the kitchen mixer, a folder of Mum's best recipes, and Dad's French holiday thrillers. On top of the trunk was a hammock and boxes of things we couldn't live without.

"Keep pushing boys!" called Dad. "A-hey! A-ho!"

He pulled the handle while Jan and I pushed. Every now and then Dad stopped and wiped his brow with his boat cap. His shirt was wet with sweat because the path up to the house was steep, and sharp stones were scattered through it. Grandpa had made the path himself.

"Stupid path," Dad muttered.

"What's that you say?" asked Grandpa.

15

He stood in front of us with the sun behind him, casting his shadow over us. The shadow was long, black and muscular, just like the boiler man he'd once knocked out on a trip over the Atlantic.

Grandpa was short and fat and had a bulgy nose.

"We're here now," said Dad.

"I may not see very well, but I'm not completely blind," replied Grandpa.

"Hello Grandpa," said my mother, because that's what she called him.

Grandpa lifted his old grey felt hat, and his bald head shone in the sunlight. He nodded, first to Mum and then to the rest of us.

"Good day to you all," he said.

That was how he talked – "Good day" and "Go'morning" – and that was as far as he went with the niceties. He replaced his hat.

"What's all that?" he shouted, pointing at the trunk. "Have you brought half of Stureby with you?"

"Just the few things we need," said Mum.

"You shouldn't bring more than you can carry!" he shouted. "Let go the handle! You boys get away!"

He put the trolley's handle to his chest and started off like a stubborn pony. His ears went red and his neck was sweating. He pulled it all by himself. We followed.

"How are you otherwise, Father?" Dad asked him.

"What do you think?" said Grandpa. "How do you think it feels to be getting old and tired?"

He complained about the snails in the strawberry patch. He swore about a holiday idiot who'd put a tent up right outside the house. Then he moaned about a bumble bee that had kept him awake half the night.

"And here you are ready to spread your belongings all over my house," he bawled. "One night I fell over a toy truck when I was on my way to the toilet. I hit my knee on the doorway and was limping like a half-wit all summer!"

He grumbled all the way up to the house, where Grandma was waiting in the kitchen. She'd been frying a pile of pancakes and had put out a jar of home-made whortleberry jam. She always did that when we arrived – but it was the only cooking she did the whole time Mum was there.

"Oh, I've been waiting for you, my darlings," said Grandma, holding out her arms.

First she hugged Dad. Then she put her arms around my brother. She took me by the hand because I was dripping water.

"Well, what shall we do when we've eaten?" she said, when we were sitting at the table. "Would you like to go down to the village to play?"

"I don't play any more," I said. "I'm going to see Klaus."

"No you're not," said Grandpa. "First you have to kill ten white-butterfly caterpillars."

Grandpa hated caterpillars. My brother and I got two kronor each for every white-butterfly caterpillar we squashed.

Grandpa hated things that buzzed, stung or irritated him. For example, he despised everything that attacked his plants. But most of all he hated the big dark stone in the middle of the strawberry patch, shadowing the delicate plants.

"I hate that lump," he said, nodding at the rock, when I gave him my bag of caterpillars.

"Why?" I asked.

"Haven't you eyes in your head? Can't you see the shadow it throws? Nothing can grow in a shadow like that."

I looked at the shadow. I didn't want to look at the bag Grandpa had put down on the ground and stamped on.

"Why don't you blow up the rock then?" I asked.

"Blow up?" said Grandpa. "No no, I'm going to get rid of it under my own steam. Now, how much money do I owe you?"

"Twenty kronor."

"I'll give it to you later," he said. "Off you go now and have some fun."

So I did.

Klaus lived with his parents on the top floor of a house in the village. Every summer he had to do something educational before he was allowed to start summer holidays properly. This was his father's idea. The year before, Klaus had to collect butterflies, find out their names, stick pins through them and put them in small boxes with glass lids. Two years ago he had to collect leaves and press them in a book.

When Klaus opened the door he looked depressed, even though I was wearing a set of false teeth from Dad's dentist practice. They gave a gleaming smile all by themselves in my mouth. But still Klaus gave me a gloomy look.

"You might as well put those away," he said. "There's no point making jokes when there's nothing to feel good about."

I put the false teeth in my pocket.

"What do you have to do this year then?" I asked. "Collect animal poo?"

"Nah, beetles," he sighed.

He said he had sixteen already.

"That's good," I said.

"Do you know how many there are in the world?"

"No," I admitted.

"Close to four-hundred thousand," said Klaus. "More than four thousand in Sweden alone."

"Cripes," I said.

"You can say that again," he said. "But I only need to collect thirty-five. And by the way I've hidden two that Dad doesn't know about – so I can have tonight off."

"Shall we go down to the jetty?" I asked.

"I reckon," he said. "But first we should each have a ciggy."

We smoked in the crevice of a rock, with a view of the lighthouse and the small islands. Farthest away was the horizon, where our gaze slipped into infinity.

"It's quite beautiful," I said.

"Is it?" said Klaus, because he'd already been on the island for a week.

"Yes," I said.

We lay in the shadow of a juniper bush, puffing on our cigarettes. It hurt my throat. I only let the smoke stay in my mouth a short time before I blew it out again. But Klaus drew deep, horrible, throat-drags. He also put out burning matches by peeing on them. Klaus had to try to do something bad every day, because his father was so strict.

"Why do I have to do something that's good for me every summer?" he asked.

"I don't know," I answered.

"It's not fair. Not when all the others are allowed to swim and sunbathe and do nothing."

"Different lots of parents are better and worse in different ways," I answered. "You can't do anything about it."

"It's not that," he said.

"I can help with the beetles if you like," I said.

"Thanks," he said and blew a smoke ring which hovered over my head like a halo. "Cool that you're here."

"Yeah," I said. "Do you know what I've been thinking?"

"No."

"That it's good to be out of town and to meet old friends again," I said.

"I think so too," said Klaus.

We stubbed out the nasty cigarettes so we could go down to the jetty. But first Klaus wanted to show me the extra beetles he'd hidden in a matchbox. One was a spit beetle and the other was a red-winged dung beetle.

"Beautiful," I said about the dung beetle.

"I found it in a cow pat," said Klaus.

"You can tell," I said.

The others were already swimming when we got to the jetty – except for Leif who had to look after his little sister, and the ones like us who didn't have bathing suits. We stood by the jetty and watched them shoving each other, hopping and diving.

"Can you see that?" I said.

"See what?" said Klaus.

"Shh!" I said.

I wanted to concentrate on Pia. She was standing on the top of the jetty in her red bathing suit. She held her arms over her head, and then she dived. She moved like a fire-red miracle through the air, into the water. It took forever for her to come back to the surface. The sun was in my eyes so tears started to run. I quickly wiped them away with my shirt.

"Aren't you going to swim?" asked Pia when she caught sight of us.

"Not today," I said. "I forgot my bathing suit."

"Doesn't matter – you usually swim in your clothes." She smiled. But she didn't laugh.

"Once a day is enough," I said.

"Do you want to come fishing soon?" she asked.

"We have to collect a lot of beetles," said Klaus with a sigh.

"Yeah, but after that?" she said, climbing back up on the jetty.

"Yeah, after that," I said.

"Let's go now," said Klaus.

When we were halfway down the jetty I turned, hoping I could see her dive again.

I couldn't get enough.

CHAPTER FOUR

I investigate Grandpa's pork chops and hug a fish

My brother and I lived in the ladies' cabin.

Grandpa and Grandma's house was made mostly of old ship cabins, which Grandpa had transported to the island on big barges. He put them together and built halls and kitchens and all the other things you need for a house. Grandpa lived in the captain's cabin, Mum and Dad lived in the back cabin and Grandma lived in the dining room.

My brother and I had the ladies' cabin, but we never admitted that to anybody, not even under torture. Instead, we said that we lived in the white salon, because our room was white except for blue window sills. Painted ships in rough seas were dotted around the walls: steam ships, yachts and warships. My favourite was a grey cannon boat in a storm.

"Twelve," I whispered.

We were lying in our bunks with our ears pricked, counting Grandpa's farts. They rumbled as if the warships on the walls had declared war and were shooting each other with their cannons.

"That one was a real boomer," said Jan.

Grandpa sounded angry even when he was asleep. We divided the farts according to a finely-tuned scale we'd made up – from the quiet mosquito-fizzers right through to the cannonball-thumpers.

"Thirteen," I said. "Looks like he's going to beat his personal best tonight."

"He should go to the Olympics," said Jan.

"Yeah, or the church choir," I said. "He's got a stomach like a set of bagpipes."

"Fourteen," counted Jan.

"That's it," I said. "He's reached his best."

"Yeah," said my brother, disappointed.

But then Grandpa farted one more time – just a tame girl-fart – but still countable, because the jury was united. We hiccupped from laughing, with our mouths buried in our pillows. Then Grandpa started to snore, discreetly at first, like an electric razor, then like a twelve horsepower outboard motor.

"That's it," said Jan.

"Yes," I said.

"By the way, do you know where to find beetles?"

"Shut up, we're going to sleep now," he said, and put his head under the pillow.

But I looked up at the ceiling and thought about Pia. In between two snores I thought I heard her hoarse laugh. But then I was already asleep.

In the days following Klaus and I looked for beetles everywhere.

We looked for bark beetles and short-winged long horns among the stumps in Grandpa's woodshed. We crept over the teacher's lawn hunting for small hard-to-find weevils. We could listen to music at the same time because the teacher played the piano with the windows open.

We kept on going, past the old bomb shelter by the road. Leif was sitting on the grass by the entrance with his little sister, putting sticks into a pile of cones.

"What are you doing?" I asked. "Making cone animals?"

"These aren't any bloody animals," he said. "These are hand grenades!"

Then he threw one at us and shouted: "Bang!" But when we'd gone a bit further away I heard him say "Moo".

"Where shall we go now?" I said.

"We'll go to Österman's compost heap and see if there's a rhino beetle there," said Klaus.

There was. It was asleep under a half-rotten cabbage leaf.

"Have you ever seen such a thing!" called Klaus. "What a piece of luck! It's a he."

He pointed to the horn at the front. It looked like a black, mini rhinoceros. Klaus said it could take five years before the larvae grew up into real insects. He also knew that they ate rotten plants and were only awake at night. He picked up the beetle and scratched its tummy to calm it down.

"Do you know what's so good about you?" I said.

"No," he said, putting the beetle in a jar of ether so it could die in peace.

"I learn so many things when I'm with you," I said. "Have we got enough beetles now?"

"Nah, we still have eight to go," he said. "Shall we take a smoko?"

"We won't have time," I said. I was thinking about Pia and how I was going fishing with her when we'd collected our beetles.

"I have to go home for lunch anyhow," he said.

I remembered that I had to too. We sat still for a minute. Klaus smoked his cigarette. He did his best to look like he was enjoying it, but breathing in the wonderful rotten smell from the compost heap was enough for me. We could hear thundering from the stable below, as if someone was banging with a big sledge hammer. But it was only Black Demon, Österman's crazy horse, kicking in the stable walls. He did it all the time. He kicked until he made a hole in the wood.

"Grandpa will have to go and bang on a couple more planks," I said.

"Sure," he said.

We carried on walking, till our roads parted.

"See you after lunch so we can carry on looking," he said.

"Yeah, I know a good stump," I said.

We decided to meet again at two o'clock.

For lunch, everyone had thick sour milk and whortle-berry jam, with hard bread crumbled on top. Except for Grandpa – he ate potatoes and two pork chops. Grandpa saved his sour milk for afternoon tea, and then he ate it with powdered ginger. He was just about to put his fork into a chop when I pulled his plate towards me. I took out my magnifying glass and looked closely at the chops.

They didn't look very good magnified. I poked them with my spoon.

"What are you doing?" shouted Grandpa.

"Yeah, what're you doing?" said my brother.

"I'm just looking to see if there are any insects here," I said.

"Why would there be any sort of insects in my chops?" asked Grandpa.

"If there were, they would be the flesh-eating beetle," I said. "They like meat. They have thorny cross bands with black spots on their cover wings."

"Oh, that sort of insect!" said Grandpa. "Can you see any?"

"No, I'm afraid not," I said.

Dad said if there were any beetles they would have died in the frypan. But it didn't make any difference. Grandpa had a new animal species to hate. He chewed as if he wanted to crush the beetles between his teeth.

I ate quickly. The grandfather clock said it was almost two o'clock.

"Ooh, I'm really full," I said. "Can I please have my caterpillar money now, Grandpa?"

"How much do I owe you?"

"Twenty kronor," I said.

He fished the coins out of his wallet. I took them and ran – I was always in a hurry in the summer. Right then I was in an extra hurry – to get to the stump.

It was the neighbour's stump by the bakery.

Klaus arrived shortly after me.

I'd told him that I was sure there would be red-winged cutter beetles in the stump. They like bark. But really I wanted to go there because Pia usually went to buy bread at that time. I had to see her, or I thought I'd go mad.

"There's nothing here," said Klaus. "Let's go."

I had another idea.

"You have to look closely," I said. "You're starting to get a little careless, Klaus."

As luck had it, Pia came past on her bicycle just at that moment. She leaned the bicycle against the fence and walked towards the bakery.

"Well hello, fancy you being here!" I said.

"How many have you got now?" she asked.

"Almost thirty," I said. "It's hot, isn't it?"

"Yes."

"Would you like an icecream?"

"If you're offering me one."

I was. I got us an icecream each, when she'd finished buying her bread. Then we stood beside her bicycle and licked our icecreams in complete harmony. I had a pistachio cone and Klaus and Pia both had vanilla.

"You know what, I had a thought," I said to Pia. "There might be other beetle species around the island.

We could come with you and go looking while you're fishing."

"Silly of me not to think of it," said Klaus.

"I only just thought of it myself," I said.

"All right then, let's do it," said Pia.

"Shall we come tomorrow?" I asked.

"Good idea," she said.

I thanked my brain for being so smart as she disappeared over the hill with the bread on her carrier.

"Thanks, brain," I whispered. "Thank you, thank you."

It was a couple of days before we could go out fishing. Pia was allowed to borrow her father's boat as often as she liked. He was an airline pilot who was always away flying around the world.

There I was, sitting in a boat, with a good friend and the girl I liked most of all in the whole world, on our way to catch beetles! Salt spray splashed my face. The sun was in our eyes. We had a bottle of orange juice and some biscuits. We didn't need to say a word, because the engine was so loud.

Things couldn't be any better.

We stopped at a medium-sized island, halfway to the horizon.

Pia stood at the end of the peninsula and cast her rod for pike, while we went around the island with our death jars and an insect net, looking for beetles. We found a pool of nasty yellow water, teeming with life.

Klaus showed me a black creepy thing with long, spindly legs, dancing on the surface of the water.

"It's a boatman," said Klaus. "It can walk on water."

"Like Jesus Christ," I said. "Get the net."

We caught it on our first try and poked it into the glass jar. We dropped some ether onto cotton balls inside the jar and then put the lid on. We could see the boatman wriggling more and more slowly with its lanky legs. After a while, it lay completely still.

"It's dead," said Klaus.

It didn't feel good.

"Why are we doing this?" I said.

"It's my father's fault," said Klaus. "Shall we go swimming now?"

But Pia didn't want to. She wanted to cast a few more times. While she was doing that we watched a couple of spinning beetles turning around and around like propellers on an old aeroplane.

We had just caught one when Pia called out, "Look!"

I passed the net to Klaus.

"You'll have to deal with the spinning beetles yourself," I said.

I wanted to give all my attention to Pia. She stood on the peninsula with her legs apart, the rod pointing to the sky. It was bending so much it looked like it was going to snap. I saw her let out more line, wind it in and let it out again. I didn't understand fishing – I never had.

But I didn't get tired of watching her.

"Get ready now, Ulf," she said.

"Ready for what?" I asked.

"Ready to grab it when it comes in," she said.

I saw the fish fight. The tail whacked the water when it hopped up for a second. Then it dived down again. All the time it was coming closer.

"What is it? A blue whale?" I wondered.

"Don't talk rubbish," she said. "Just grab it!"

I saw the green shadow on the bottom. I splashed in with my clothes on, again. Somehow I succeeded in getting my hands around the fish. It twisted and turned, and it opened its mouth so I could see all its needle-sharp teeth. I tried not to look into its hideous eyes.

"I've got it!" I puffed.

I took a couple of steps towards land. But just when I was about to climb out of the water, the wily pike hit my left knee. I lost my balance and slipped on the slimy, soap-slippery rocks. I fell and hit my right eyebrow on the rocks. My head filled with angry blue stars. I scraped both my elbows, but I didn't let go. The pike went quiet. It probably fainted when I fell on top of it. Somehow I managed to get myself up onto the beach, and I placed the pike like a sacrifice at Pia's feet.

"Here you are," I said.

"You're bleeding," she said.

She hit the unconscious pike on the head. Then she turned to me.

"Lie on your back," she said.

When the stars in my head had quietened down, I could see the summer clouds moving in the sky. An osprey was circling high above, like a vulture that can smell a half-dead hero.

"How do you feel?" she asked.

"I'm fine," I said.

Then I had a better thought.

"Apart from my whole head buzzing like a beehive," I added. "I don't think I can stand up."

She bent her face over me. I looked into her brown eyes and I didn't ever want to come out again. Then she wrinkled her brow and let her cold fingers brush my split eyebrow. They felt like the healing fingers of Mother Teresa and they smelled of fish.

"You don't need stitches," she said.

Klaus came with the orange juice and the biscuits. He parked the packet on my stomach.

"You can have them all," he said, as if it was my last supper, and then he went back to his beetles.

"Thanks," I said, exhausted.

"Lie very still," said Pia. "You might have a small concussion. I'm going to stop the bleeding."

She took her pink towel, dipped it in the sea water and pressed it against the cut. She laid the rest of the towel over my face. It's the same towel she's dried herself with, I thought. The thought made me dizzy. I breathed in her smell. It was sweet and sour, like tea with honey and lemon. I held my breath as long as I could.

"Hold the towel yourself while I clean the pike," she said, when at last I breathed out. "Thanks for grabbing it. It must weigh more than six kilos, don't you think?"

"Has to," I said.

After a while I lifted the towel so I could see her. She was squatting by a rock. She cut the pike's stomach open with a knife and pulled out the innards – placing one bit beside the other in a tidy row.

"Here's the spleen," she said. "And here's the stomach … and the kidney and the swim bladder that lets the fish decide how deep it should swim… and here's the heart."

"You know a lot," I said.

"I'm going to be a theatre nurse," she said.

I lay and admired her surgical talents. With her index finger she pulled out the membranes still in the stomach and then rinsed it out with sea water. Her white-clothed assistants, the gulls and terns, circled around her head waiting for abandoned organs. But I was concentrating on the pike's heart, which lay on the ground in front of me, beating and beating even though it was dead.

My own heart was beating and beating too.

"Do you like me?" I asked Pia, without thinking.

I lifted my head for safety's sake, in case she wanted to kiss me.

"Looks like you really did get concussion," she said.

Then she threw the pike into the boat. I took a mouthful of orange juice so I could pretend nothing had happened and passed the bottle to Pia.

"Can't you laugh a little," I said.

"Why should I laugh?" she asked.

"Because I want you to," I said.

"But I don't have anything to laugh at," she said.

We didn't stay long after that. Pia had her giant fish, so she was pleased. Klaus had two new dead beetles, so he was pleased too. I had a cut eyebrow and heartburn. I was the most pleased of anybody.

CHAPTER FIVE

I am reminded of something I had forgotten

A couple of days later I was lying on the sofa bed in the back cabin where Mum and Dad slept at night. I loved lying there watching the specks of dust falling and falling for eternity, in the light from the window. I pretended they were planets and moons, floating through space.

I had a plaster over one eye, which made me look tough and experienced in the ways of the world.

"My dear boy, what have you done?" Mum had asked when I came home with my cut eyebrow.

"Have you been in a fight?" Grandpa asked with interest.

"Yes," I said.

"With a fish," said Klaus, who'd followed me home.

My brother thought this was funny. Sometimes Klaus is not very sensitive. Dad reluctantly pulled himself out of the hammock; left his crossword, washed my wound with 96 percent dental spirit, and put a plaster on it. Then he went back to his hammock and his crossword. He chewed the end of a pencil and scratched his ear. He called this 'resting up'.

"'A jammed cylinder'," he read.

"How many letters?" asked Mum.

"Five and then four," said Dad.

"I know what it is," said Mum.

"Me too," said my brother.

"You don't know, either of you," said Dad. "You can both be quiet."

I went into the salon and looked at myself in the mirror. I thought about what might be funny enough to make Pia laugh. Next day I climbed down into the cellar and collected twenty old magazines. They had articles on natural science, terrible tales about war, and funny stories called *Humour in Uniform*.

I'd always laughed at them.

I had fun now too. I lay and giggled to myself, while I learned one of the stories off by heart. After that I stood in front of the mirror, practising it.

Once there was a soldier who got a stone in his shoe, I began.

The telephone rang in the hall. A moment later Mum came into the cabin without knocking.

"You're laughing," she said.

"Yes, I'm learning funny stories," I said. "Do you want to hear one?"

"No, not just now. There's something I have to talk to you about. Something not so funny. Do you know who it was who rang just now?"

"No."

"It was Percy's mother. She was in a very good mood."

"Oh no," I sighed.

"She was very pleased," said Mum. "Do you know why? She is happy that Percy is coming here, so she and her husband will be able to go camping together just like they did when they were young. She asked what Percy should bring with him when he comes tomorrow."

"Tomorrow?" I said.

"Yes, exactly, tomorrow," said Mum. "But why in heaven's name have you not said anything, child?"

"I forgot," I said. "I've had so much else to think about."

And that was true.

Love makes you remember some things which otherwise you'd forget – a look, a dive, a laugh, the smell of a beach towel. But it makes you forget other things completely – such as inviting your best friend to your cantankerous grandfather's house on an island.

I didn't even know if I wanted Percy to come any more. He would disturb the beetle-collecting and the love.

Mum shook her head.

"Some things you cannot forget," she said. "If Percy's mother hadn't sounded so exorbitantly happy I would have said no straight away."

"Yes," I said.

"But what could I say?" she continued. "I was taken completely off guard. And it's your birthday tomorrow and everything."

"Is it?" I said.

"Don't be stupid," said Mum. "We'll talk about this at dinner."

She left the room. I fished out the false teeth and put them in my mouth. When I looked at myself in the mirror the teeth smiled all by themselves. I looked really funny. Ha, ha!

I laughed as loud a laugh as I could to cheer myself up. I'd never forgotten my birthday before.

After that I went out and collected twelve white-butterfly caterpillars in a bag and gave them to Grandpa for no pay. I collected two buckets of water from the well. I ran to the shop and bought a packet of cigarettes for Grandma. And I offered to help Dad with the crossword. He said no.

In spite of all my efforts, the atmosphere was not the best at dinner. The school teacher was practising a funeral hymn in the house next door. Grandpa chewed his pork chops. The rest of us had cod with egg sauce, and grated horseradish if we wanted. Grandma ate the cod head. She poked hungrily at the cooked brains with her fork.

"What? Is Percy coming here?" asked my brother. "Where will the idiot stay? Isn't it bad enough that I have to share a room with this lump of lard?"

He pointed at me with his knife.

"That'll do, Jan," said Dad. "Ulf is not fat – he's just sturdy. But I must say, he hasn't handled this business very well. Ulf, you cannot just unilaterally decide things like this. You understand that, don't you?"

"Yes," I said, even though I didn't know what uni-laterally meant. I could tell that it wasn't anything good.

"Is someone else coming here?" shrieked Grandpa, who didn't hear very well, especially when he was concentrating on his dinner.

"Yes, a school friend of Ulf's," said Mum in a loud voice. "A very nice boy. His name is Percy. He's coming on the twelve o'clock boat."

"Another snotty puppy," shouted Grandpa so that sauce sprayed from his mouth. "What do you think this is? A hostel for badly brought-up children? I can say this much – if he annoys me, he'll be on the next boat home, do you hear me?"

"Why do you always have to shout like that?" asked Grandma.

"Because," said Grandpa, chewing on nothing, "because, because… so I can be in peace!"

He went out, holding his chops in his hand.

Grandma smoothed back a piece of beautiful white hair that had fallen across her forehead. Then she sucked on a boiled cod eye. She thought it was the best bit. I thought it was worse than a horror movie. But right then I was thinking about Percy.

He had managed to annoy everyone before he'd even got here.

"It's still my birthday tomorrow," I said quietly.

"Yeah, there'll hardly be any presents for you," said my brother.

"There aren't usually very many anyway," I said.

It was true. That was the worst thing about having a birthday in summer. There's not much you can buy in the way of a present at the corner store. I usually finished up with a drawing pad, a packet of crayons, a piece of cheese and a cake of chocolate. Every year I asked for cheese. I love cheese. Sometimes Mum and Dad also brought something for me from town.

"I'm giving you a horse bite for your birthday," my brother whispered to me.

A horse bite is when someone grabs hold of the skin under your leg and twists it.

"Thanks," I said.

"Yes, thanks for dinner," said Dad. "It was really good." He said that even though he'd only eaten half of what was on his plate.

Mum did the dishes and Dad went back to his never-ending crossword. Grandma put herself in her favourite chair by the window. She looked out over the trees and the water, smoking a cigarette in a long holder.

The smoke swirled its way up to the ceiling, as white as her fluffy hair, which was arranged in something Mum called a piggy back – though it was lovely.

She had a straight back and looked like someone in a French film.

"Can you blow a smoke ring?" I asked.

She did it without answering. I stood behind her looking out the window. Grandpa was out there in his stained old hat digging up more stones. He did it all the time. He threw them away, so he'd have more dirt for his garden.

He was tossing the earth over his shoulder with angry, staccato movements.

"Grandma," I said.

"Yes, what is it dear?" she said.

"I'm just wondering why Grandpa is always so angry."

"He is as he is," she said.

"Has he always been angry?"

"Nay, not at first maybe," she said, after a while. "Not in the beginning when we first met... he was happy then. He probably hoped I would start to like him as much as he liked me."

"And you didn't?"

She didn't answer. She just sent up another smoke signal.

"But why did you marry him then?"

"You know what your Grandpa is like."

"How do you mean?"

"Stubborn," said Grandma. "When he's got some-thing into his head he doesn't give up. And I probably thought that he would be away so much because he worked at sea."

"Wasn't he away, then?"

"Yes," said Grandma. "Yes, he was... and after every trip he came home with presents he'd made. He looked at me and hoped I'd be happy. But how can anyone look happy when they aren't?"

"I don't know."

"No, how could you? I only hope things go well with your wee friend," said Grandma.

"I hope so too," I said.

I went to bed early. I tried to dream that I was telling Pia a funny story and that she laughed and laughed till she fell into my arms. But it didn't work. I dreamed about Percy instead. He stood in the front of an archipelago boat and waved and called out.

"Here I come, Ulf!" he called.

"Oh, cripes," I thought.

CHAPTER SIX

Percy arrives and Grandpa demolishes a chair

The next day Percy arrived on the twelve o'clock boat. It was windy and raining. I stood on the jetty and waited, with Grandma's umbrella over my head. Percy stood up the front and waved.

"Here I come, Ulf!" he shouted long before the boat had docked.

I wasn't sure whether to be happy or sad.

He was wearing a pair of cut-off trousers, sandals, a jacket, and he had quite a small bag. He was also wearing a cork belt around his waist.

"Crikey, it's great to be here," he said, when he'd hopped onto land. "I've been waiting and waiting. Mum baked a tiger cake for us. And I borrowed this from my cousin."

He pointed proudly at his cork belt.

"Have you been wearing that the whole trip?" I asked.

"Yes, 'cos you don't want to drown, do you, for crissakes," he said. "I told Dad I would learn to swim twenty metres. 'I'd like to see that,' he said. We had a twenty kronor bet. What do you reckon about that?"

I said nothing.

We boxed each other in the stomach for a joke because it was so long since we'd been together. We went past the shelter. Inside it I'd carved a heart. And inside the heart:

ULF + PIA = TRUE LOVE

I'd carved it under the bench so that no one would be able to see it.

I'd also written on the wall:

IF YOUR HEART SHOULD EVER BREAK
FIX IT UP WITH SELLOTAPE

But I didn't show it to Percy. We sloped past the old wreck slowly rotting in the bay and went up the steep hill towards the house.

Percy pulled his cap over his ears and his teeth chattered.

"It almost always rains on my birthday," I said, apologetically.

"That's right, happy birthday," he chattered. "I didn't bring a present. I was sort of thinking that I could be the present."

"You are, too," I said. "Now we'll go and say hello to Grandpa. But remember what I've told you."

"What have you told me?"

"That you have to be careful around him, because he goes crazy when he gets angry."

"Don't worry," said Percy, and put his arm around my shoulders. "Is it far to go?"

"No, here it is!" I said.

We'd passed the top of the hill, and there was the white house in front of our noses. Percy put his bag in a puddle. He gazed at the two towers, called turrets, and he admired the flat-roofed bridge between them.

"This is not a house, Ulf," he said. "This is a castle."

"Call it what you like," I said. "Let's go inside."

Grandpa had been kneeling on his bad knee in the pouring rain picking strawberries for the cake. He didn't like cake.

And he didn't like getting wet either.

He was going to have his sour milk.

We sat in the front room listening to the grandfather clock's never-ending ticking and the never-ending drumming of the rain on the roof.

The grown-ups drank coffee. The non-grown-ups had raspberry cordial.

48

When we'd sat down Grandpa pointed at Percy with his thick index finger.

"So, you must be Percy," he said.

"Yes," said Percy.

"You look all right," said Grandpa. "You can get me a bowl of sour milk. It's in the fridge on the landing. You'll find a bowl in the kitchen cupboard, spoons in the drawer. I'd like a dessertspoon of sugar in it and a good amount of ginger. The spice jars are on the shelf. Hurry up, boy!"

"Aye aye, Captain," said Percy, though Grandpa had been chief engineer.

After a bit of clatter he came back with Grandpa's bowl and gave him a salute.

"Don't be silly," said Grandpa. "Put some cake in your mouth to keep it quiet!"

While Percy was in the kitchen Mum had lit the candles on the cake. I blew them out in a single breath, like you're supposed to. That meant you could wish for something. I knew exactly what it was.

"What did you wish for, Ulf?" asked Grandma.

"You aren't allowed to say it out loud, because then it won't work," I said.

"But it starts with K and ends with two S's and it has an I in the middle," said my brother, drumming his spoon on the saucer.

"No it doesn't," I said. "I wished for a steamroller so I can drive over you."

"Don't fight boys," said Dad. "Remember I'm on holiday."

I liked the cake – it had cream on top. Mum had baked it herself. Everyone except for Grandpa enjoyed eating it. Grandpa had his sour milk and ginger. Then he sneezed. He sneezed so hard, the strawberries almost blew off the cake. Then he carried on sneezing. His face got redder. In the end he looked like a strawberry, with his round head with no hair except for a few tufts by his ears.

"Was this your idea?" Grandpa said to Percy, when he'd finished sneezing.

"What's that?" asked Percy.

"Don't try to get out of it," said Grandpa. "Someone put pepper instead of ginger in my sour milk. Was it you?"

"Yes," said Percy.

"He must've got the wrong jar," I said. "He's never been here before."

"I didn't take the wrong jar," said Percy. "It was a joke."

Grandpa got out of his chair and stared at Percy.

"Are you not afraid of me?" he yelled.

"No," said Percy, and he stood up as well.

"You are not supposed to annoy me!" shouted Grandpa, stamping his foot.

"Has Grandpa not got a sense of humour?" said Percy.

Then Grandpa lifted his chair over his head. It was an oak chair – a strong, old chair with a carved lion's head on the back, a leather seat and lion paws on its legs.

"Are you afraid now?" shouted Grandpa.

"No," said Percy.

Grandpa slammed the chair on the table so hard that the wood split. The coffee cups and glasses jumped and the chair legs broke off. My brother went white. Dad went pale too.

There was silence.

"Well? That must have frightened you," said Grandpa.

"Nope," said Percy.

I almost didn't dare to look at Grandpa. But I couldn't help it. His nostrils were flaring. His jaw was clenched so hard you could hear his teeth grinding. Even the white-powdered ladies in the painting hung above the sofa looked a bit nervous. But not Percy. He put his chin up.

Then Grandpa laughed.

"You're a brave lad," he said. "Now we'll go to the workshop and fix the chair."

I went along as well. In the workshop Grandpa had thousands of tools and things which might be useful: saws, chisels, spanners, tractor tyres, sieves, sledge-hammers, twine, spades, cement, crowbars, copper wire, tar paper, and two drawers full of bent nails that he banged out straight when he was in the mood.

They tried to fit the chair legs together on the work-bench.

"That was a real bang, eh?" smiled Grandpa.

"Yeah, the best I've ever heard," said Percy. "Shall I put a screw in here?"

"Just what I was thinking," said Grandpa.

They glued the legs together. I helped as well. Grandpa seemed pleased to have two assistants. When we were finished it had stopped raining.

A rainbow shone over the fjord, as if it wanted to celebrate my birthday.

"We've done very well," said Grandpa, and he patted Percy on the shoulder. "If you have any spare time, you can always straighten out some nails."

"Yeah, that sounds fun," said Percy.

When we came back Jan was drying the dishes. He gave Percy a sour look and pretended to talk to two flies buzzing about the oven.

"I'm going to have to share a room with that idiot," he said.

The flies said nothing.

"It doesn't matter. I can sleep anywhere," said Percy. "I've done it before."

"You can sleep in my room," said Grandpa.

"Thank you," said Percy.

Behind him, my brother stood and giggled, holding his nose.

CHAPTER SEVEN

We find faith, hope and love in the woodshed

Percy wanted me to show him around so he could see what things were like on an island. I showed him the long drop where spiders had woven lace curtains over the window, and the cellar, and the wardrobe which smelled of mothballs, and the cabin-rifle hidden behind Grandma's old winter coat. Then we went to the fallen-down shed at the beach, and looked at the rotten sailing canoe.

"Dad built it when he was young," I said.

"Shall we fix it up?" asked Percy.

"Not possible," I said. "Now we'll go to the woodshed."

So we did. There was a chopping stump outside with an axe in it, and a pile of uncut wood. Inside the shed, something shone in the light from the door.

"What's that?" Percy asked.

"What?" I said.

"That thing that's shiny," he said.

I knew what it was. Grandpa didn't want to talk about it. But Dad had told me.

"It's everything Grandpa made for Grandma when he was at sea."

"I want to see it," said Percy.

Percy always wanted to see shiny things.

So we pulled it all out. There was a table with the top made of copper which Grandpa had hammered so it was buckly. The legs were made of brass. And even though the metal had lost most of its shine, it still looked impressive. On the short sides Grandpa had bent some thin brass pipes so they made Grandma's initials: E S – Erika Stark.

Also hidden amongst the wood was a four-leaf clover made of copper, with a cross, an anchor and a heart of brass.

"That means faith, hope and love," I said.

On the leaves of the clover there were oval photographs. Engraved in swirly letters were the words, *To Erika on her birthday*.

"Who's that?" Percy nodded at the photo.

"Grandpa and Grandma when they were young," I said. "Don't you think the copper clover is just so ugly?"

But Percy admired Grandpa's metalwork. He studied every tiny screw.

"Look at the turned handles," he said. "It must have taken forever to make."

"Possibly," I said. "But it's still not beautiful. And Grandma didn't want it. She hid it out here. Let's put it back."

But we didn't have time – Grandpa arrived with a branch to saw up. He dropped it and stared at the table and the copper clover.

He swallowed and rubbed his forehead.

"What are you up to?" he asked quietly. "All that scrap should go. Take it away! I don't want to see it!"

"I think it's beautiful. I can polish it up," said Percy.

"That's the last straw," shouted Grandpa. "What did I say? Away! Off you go!"

When we had walked away a bit we turned around. We saw Grandpa lift up the table and throw it in through the door with all his strength. And the clover with the photographs flew after. Then we went into the house.

"Now you've made Grandpa angry twice today," I said. "Why did you put pepper in his sour milk?"

"I took the wrong jar," said Percy. "It was a mistake. But I thought it seemed cowardly to say so."

That evening we played Black Peter three times, because I'd said that we usually played games on the island. My brother played too, because it was my birthday. He got to shuffle, because he had bought the cards.

I'd already been Black Peter twice.

Then I was again.

"How strange," said my brother. "What bad luck! You're not sad about it are you?"

"No," I said. "I've grown out of that."

"Then let's play one more time," said my brother.

"No, that will be enough," called Grandpa from the captain's cabin. "I want to sleep. And I hate card games. Come here, Percy. You too, Ulf!"

We were sent off to get a rubber mattress from the wardrobe. We blew it up till we were dizzy and put it on Grandpa's floor, where Percy was going to sleep. Then we untied Grandpa's shoelaces for him. He found it so hard to reach. When he was at sea he had a special boy who tied and untied his shoelaces.

"My stomach gets in the way," he said. "Do you think I'm fat?"

"Yes," said Percy.

"You're right," said Grandpa. "But now I'll show you something!"

He went over to the writing desk. It had three drawers, but one was locked. I knew that because I'd tried to open it several times. Now he blew on his fist, and when he opened it he was holding a key. I had never seen him do that trick before. He unlocked the drawer and took some money out of it.

"Do you know what this is, Percy?" he asked.

"Of course he does," I said. "It's money."

"Yes, but not just any sort of money," said Grandpa. "It's a silver dollar. Not just any old silver dollar – a special one. Do you see this?"

He put his thumbnail in the middle of the coin.

"There's a buckle there," said Percy.

"That's where Buffalo Bill shot it," said Grandpa.

Then he told us about Buffalo Bill.

It was the first time I'd heard Grandpa talk about him. And for once in his life, he almost never swore at all.

His real name was William F Cody, said Grandpa. He called himself Buffalo Bill because he thought it sounded better and because he was a famous buffalo hunter and adventurer in the Wild West.

"I saw him when I was in London," said Grandpa. "He was there with his Wild West circus which travelled around the world. I went three times."

"Was it good?" asked Percy.

"Good?" said Grandpa. "It was wonderful! Wild buffalo rushed towards you so fast you thought they'd end up in your lap. The place was full of Indians and cowboys. I'd never seen anything like it. Buffalo Bill sat on a white horse and he was the best shot by far. People threw coins in the air and he shot holes in them. I caught this one."

Grandpa turned the coin. He sent it spinning up in the air and caught it.

"I wouldn't sell this for anything," he said. "It's a memory. I asked him afterwards if he wanted it back. 'No, no,' he said. 'Just keep it.'"

"So you really talked to him?" I said.

"Absolutely," said Grandpa. "And I shook his hand as well. He had white gloves. 'Nice to meet you,'" he said.

He smiled. Then he put the coin back in the drawer.

"I got a photo of him," Grandpa said, "on his horse. I asked him to write something to Grandma on it. He wrote: *To Erika Stark with love, yours, Buffalo Bill.* I don't know if she still has it. But she said she'd never seen a better-looking man."

"Why haven't you told me this before?" I asked.

It felt unfair. First Percy came here and annoyed him, and now Grandpa was telling him all his secrets.

"I don't know. It just hasn't happened," said Grandpa.

"No, it hasn't," I said.

"I'd really like to read you his memoirs," he said. "It's the best book there is. But my eyes are so bad. Can you read out loud for us, Percy?"

"I don't see why not," said Percy.

Grandpa went and got William F Cody's memoirs and Percy began to read.

At school he usually stammered and lost his place when he had to read out loud. But now he read as fluently as anything, with a real radio voice. He read about when Buffalo Bill was little and his papa moved the family to Kansas and annoyed some slave owners so that he got stabbed in the back.

Percy continued: *I thought he was mortally wounded. The knife had gone into his kidneys and left a terrible wound. He didn't die from it – Mama looked after him carefully. But this was only the beginning.*

Grandpa began to snore. He sounded like a panting buffalo beast. Percy lay down on the rubber mattress and put the book under his head.

"Good reading," I said. "See you tomorrow."

"Your Grandpa is fun," said Percy.

"Do you think so?"

"Yep. Angry and fun."

"He's a bit of both," I said. "Goodnight."

I sneaked into the ladies' cabin and climbed onto the top bunk.

"He will be but a short time on this earth, your friend," said my brother from the bottom bunk. "Grandpa will soon fart him to bits."

"He'll manage," I said. "But you have to be quiet now so I can do my dreaming."

I wanted to dream about… guess who?

I woke up twice in the night when the school teacher coughed in the house next door. I tried to remember Pia's smell.

But how can you remember a smell?

It is almost impossible.

Especially if you sleep in a room next to Grandpa.

CHAPTER EIGHT

We spy on nudists and a beetle is born

The next day Percy wasn't in the house when I woke up.

He'd found a place to sleep outside in the hammock in front of the house – rolled up like a cocoon in Grandma's winter coat. He had an old fur muff as a pillow and Grandma's white hat on his head.

He was lying on his back listening to the school teacher playing an early morning concert on his piano.

"Hello Ulf," he said without looking at me. "Did you sleep well?"

"Why are you lying out here?" I asked. "Couldn't you manage one night with Grandpa?"

"What do you mean, manage?" he said. "I just wanted to look at the stars. The night sky is completely different on an island. Absolutely black! You can see right out to space. What shall we do today?"

He wanted to do something all the time.

He'd already chopped wood and collected water.

"We can row out to sea," I said. "That's the sort of thing you do on an island. But first we'll have some breakfast."

"Can't we eat at sea?" said Percy. "That would make it quicker."

"I don't see why not," I said.

We took drinks and the tiger cake Percy had brought with him from home; we also had Grandpa's binoculars. We ran down to the bay. Percy had the cork belt around his waist, because he'd promised his mother not to drown.

"I'm an only child, you see," he said. "Where will we get a boat?"

We borrowed Österman's dinghy, because no one rowed it anymore. I hope with all my heart that none of my friends are here, I thought. I was lucky. There was no one in sight when we jumped on board. Actually I was worrying about what it would be like when Percy met them. He was the best friend you could have. But he could be really hard work.

"You don't need to speak if we meet anyone," I said.

"Why not?" he asked.

"Because that's not what you do when you're on an island," I said.

We cast off – except we didn't get very far, because Percy wanted to row the whole time. He splashed the oars like an idiot and the dinghy spun around and around. All the time his face was shining with pure happiness.

"This is going really well!" he yelled. "When did you learn to row?"

"When I was five," I said. "Think about what you're doing with the blades of the oars!"

It didn't take long before Pia popped up on the beach. She was out walking her family's red-eyed cocker spaniel. She stopped and looked at us while the dog lapped up a few tongues of sea water.

"How is your head feeling today, then?" she yelled. "And who have you got with you in the boat?"

I pretended I couldn't hear.

But Percy stood up and waved with one of the oars.

"It's ME!" he yelled. "My name is Percy!"

I grabbed the oars and rowed away with quick strokes. Pia was still watching us. She held her hand over her eyes like an Indian. It looked like both she and the dog were laughing.

"Who's that girl?" asked Percy.

"Her name is Pia," I said. "And there's nothing special about her."

"Yes there is," said Percy. "But don't worry about it. Let's eat."

We lay down and let the boat drift wherever it wanted to.

Happy white clouds floated above and the tiger cake was dry but good. We took turns to drink out of a hip flask full of milk.

"What a helluva fantastic summer this is going to be," said Percy.

"Hope so," I said.

"I am going to do EVERYTHING people do when they're on an island. What did you like doing best when you were little?"

I had to think about that. I thought about everything I'd done: the home-made raft which had almost drifted out to sea; the kites we flew high up towards the sun; the rush to the stomach I got when I jumped in Samuelsson's barn; the times we had frightened the living daylights out of the midwife on dark evenings.

"Probably being an Indian," I said at last. "Spying on people and things."

"Then let's do that."

"But it was a thousand years ago," I protested. "I was only little."

"But I never got to do it when I was little."

What can you say to that? We rowed to an island and found a duck feather and another one from a seagull.

"I am Happy Cloud," said Percy, putting the duck feather behind his ear. "Who are you?"

"Big Bum," I said, wanting to sound stupid.

But I put the seagull feather behind my ear anyway. It didn't feel too stupid. I remembered my life as an Indian, how we'd set fire to Grandpa's straw mattress and made smoke signals with a blanket till the volunteer fire brigade turned up, and how we hunted Ericsson's cows with a lasso and fought battles till the tomato sauce flowed.

Those were the days.

"Now we should start spying," said Percy. "Who shall we spy on?"

I knew.

I rowed quietly into the fjord.

"Not a sound now," I whispered. The boat glided into the reeds lining the beach, with a swishing sound.

I gave him Grandpa's binoculars and pointed to a brown-stained house, twenty-five metres away at most. A couple of nudists lived there. That meant they went around with no clothes on. The man sat in a cane chair reading a book, while the woman was hanging out the washing. She was wearing a shawl on her head, but otherwise she was completely naked. She pointed her round bottom towards us.

Percy gave a whistle.

The binoculars were so strong that you could see even the tiniest strand of hair.

"Fantastic binnies," he said.

"Haven't you finished looking?" I said, after a while.

"Not quite," he said. "She needs to turn around first."

I didn't think it was exciting now. I'd seen it too many times. They were skinny and middle-aged and they looked completely normal. But this was the first time for Percy. Suddenly the woman turned towards us so you could see her breasts. They looked like the ones Eve had in Grandma's *Illustrated Bible*.

"Man – these pale faces are so pale. Over their whole bodies," he whispered.

"We're going now," I said.

He put the binoculars away. I started to back out. But before we disappeared Percy wanted to call out a greeting to the pale faces.

So he did.

"THANKS FOR THE LOOK!" he shouted. "THERE WASN'T MUCH TO SEE!"

I rowed back so fast my throat was dry.

On our way to the shop, who should we meet, on the hill? Klaus!

"I was just on my way to see you Ulf," he said. "What on earth were you doing yesterday? I was waiting for you. Were you sick?"

"Nah, we ate strawberry cake because it was his birthday," said Percy. "Then we fixed a chair and read a book called *Buffalo Bill*."

"Excuse me, but who are you?" asked Klaus.

"I'm Percy," said Percy. "I am Ulf's best friend. We're blood brothers. And who are you?"

Klaus didn't answer. But he put his finger over one nostril and shot a projectile of snot from the other. He was good at it.

"He's called Klaus," I explained. "He's my best friend on the island. He's a damned good guy, actually. He smokes Chesterfields and collects beetles."

Percy wiped his right hand on his trouser leg.

Then he stuck it out towards Klaus.

"Any friend of Ulf's is a friend of mine," he said. "How many beetles have you got?"

It was a miracle. They shook hands. Except neither looked the other in the eyes. They were both looking at me.

"Thirty-four," Klaus sighed.

"He has to get thirty-five before he can be free and have summer holidays," I said. "It's his father's rules."

"He must be crazy," said Percy.

Klaus kicked a stone.

"They all are," Percy continued. "My father's strange too. Come on. We're going to buy sweets."

We went into the shop and bought a bag of sweets and two bottles of fizzy. We breathed in the smell of herrings, kerosene and insect repellent. Klaus bought me a *Phantom* for my birthday and then he said he'd never find the last stupid beetle. He'd looked everywhere.

"And tomorrow we were going to play kick-the-can," he said.

"Don't worry. I'll fix it," said Percy, offering him a sweet.

"How?" said Klaus.

"Don't you have any imagination? Let's go to your place and look at the beetles."

It didn't take very long to get to where Klaus lived up the hill. But Kicki, Pia and Gunn Britt were standing by the postbox giggling and reading each other's postcards out loud to each other. They looked up. Pia was wearing a red jersey. I had no idea what the others were wearing.

"Why have you got feathers on your heads?" giggled Pia.

"We haven't," I said, feeling my head. "Yes we do – that's strange!"

I plucked my feather off. But Percy let his stay.

"We're Indians," Percy said. "I'm Happy Cloud and he is Big Bum. We've just been spying on a pair of nudies."

My ears went as red as a redskin.

The girls giggled.

When we were out of earshot I said to Percy, "I told you not to speak to anyone."

We sat round the table in Klaus's room. He'd put out all the bits of cardboard he had stuck beetles onto. On the corner of each he'd printed their Swedish and Latin names in tiny letters. Percy admired every beetle leg and every eye facet through a magnifying glass.

"They're beautiful," he said.

"Do you think so?" asked Klaus.

"Yeah, but the gold beetle is the most beautiful."

"The rhino beetle is pretty cool," I said.

"You could play soldiers with them," said Percy.

Klaus got a worried wrinkle in his forehead.

"We won't bother with that," he said. "So how will you find the last beetle, since you've got such a good imagination?"

Percy tapped his forehead.

"Do you have any extras?" he asked.

"Yeah," said Klaus. "But it won't help. It has to be a new one. Dad knows every single beetle there is."

"I doubt it," said Percy.

He asked Klaus to bring out his supply of reserve beetles, as well as a needle, a knife, some cutters and a tube of glue.

"What are you going to do?" asked Klaus.

"You'll see."

Percy had always been good at crafts. He whistled cheerfully while he cut the head off a carrion beetle. Then he cut the back end off an abandoned biting buck. He nipped the head of the pin off and then he joined the two parts together using the pin as a graft between them. To be safe, he poked in some Karlson's glue as well.

"If your heart should ever stew, fix it up with Karlson's glue," I said.

"That's right," said Percy, looking at the result. "Here's your last beetle. It just needs to dry."

"What sort is it?" I asked, just so he could say something clever.

"A rescue summer beetle," said Percy. "It's going to make your Dad go nuts, Klaus."

Klaus turned the masterpiece over and over. His eyes were shining.

"I'll be blowed," he said.

He slapped Percy several times on the back and offered him his father's last two Chesterfields.

"You're a genius. And tomorrow I get to play kick-the-can!"

"What kind of can?" asked Percy.

'You'll see," I said. "We have to go home for lunch now."

"Ugh!" said Happy Cloud.

CHAPTER NINE

We see Sweden's most angry horse

"Nice guy, that Klaus," said Percy.

"Sure," I said.

I didn't like it that Percy had made friends with Klaus straight away. And I didn't understand why I didn't like it. Before I'd been worrying that they wouldn't like each other when they met. Now they were friends and I still wasn't happy.

Why was that?

Was I turning into a teenager?

We sat on the hill eating the baked ginger apples Mum had made for dessert. I tried not to show my feelings. We watched the ships sailing past in the fjord, and guessed which country each came from, and we killed a few afternoon mosquitoes.

"What a day!" said Percy. "That was really fun playing Indians. What else did you do when you were little, Ulf?"

"I'm not going to tell you if you rush around telling everybody."

"Why would I do that?" asked Percy.

"You might forget and do it," I said.

"Do you want a fight?" he asked.

He boxed me hard on the shoulder. I felt better straight away. So I told him that me and my friends had built a lot of huts through the years. Sometimes we built them in trees, sometimes on the ground.

"Let's build one with a sea view," said Percy. "Up here on the hill. Let's start now – so we can stay in it tonight."

Grandpa had rebuilt the jetty not so long ago. He'd left a whole lot of old planks, so there was plenty of wood for us to use. Tools and everything else we needed were in the workshop.

We were about to start heaving it all up the hill when Grandpa came up.

"Where do you think you're going with my workshop, you slugs?" he shouted.

But he wasn't shouting in a nasty way.

"Percy wants to build a hut we can sleep in," I said.

"Ah ha, so you think I fart too much at night?" said Grandpa.

"Not exactly," Percy answered politely.

"Tell it straight," said Grandpa. "There's a cauldron

of gases in my stomach. Erika couldn't stand it either...
if that's what it was."

He spat and threw a bag of cement onto his back.
Then he pointed to a hammer, a pile of planks and a lot
more things. He told us to put everything into a beer
crate.

"Carry," he said. "You have to do something for your
food and board!"

"Where are we going?" I asked.

"To Österman's," said Grandpa. "I'm going to fix his
stable, because his horse has kicked the wall down
again. If you help me with that, I'll help you with the
hut later."

"Deal," said Percy.

He even shook hands on it. He was going to be a
businessman after all.

We helped as much as we could. Percy, who was a
handyman, was allowed to hammer some plank-ends
to strengthen the wall. I mixed the cement, which
Grandpa then spread on the base that had cracked.
The whole time we worked, we could hear the horse
stamping and snorting inside. Every now and again it
neighed a terrible neigh and kicked the wall so the
planks bowed.

"What a toughy! Won't he ever get tired?" asked Percy.

"Never," I said. "Black Demon is the angriest horse in Sweden. He kicks down the stable at least two times a year. Kalle who owns him is the only man brave enough to go in and give him food. And you can never let him out to graze."

"I have to see him," said Percy.

When we looked through the gap in the door Percy had to draw breath. There was Black Demon! He was big and dirty and terrifying. It looked like he was radiating the light beams streaming in through the gaps in the stable walls. Then he turned towards us. The whites of his eyes gleamed. His ears were pinned back. He showed his long yellow teeth. When his muscles flexed under the skin, a cloud of dust rose.

"There, there old boy," said Percy. "Don't be afraid. It's just me, Percy."

Then Black Demon neighed and kicked out one of the new planks.

"What the hell are you doing, boys!" called Grandpa. "You're not committing suicide?"

"I was just saying hello to Black Demon," said Percy.

"Well don't," said Grandpa. "Otherwise we'll never get finished."

He fixed the plank that Black Demon had just kicked out. Then it was time to pick up our things.

"Why is Black Demon so angry?" Percy asked.

"Who knows what's going on inside the head of a horse?" said Grandpa. "Or inside the head of a person for that matter. Maybe the devil horse had its heart broken. Maybe it hoped for something that didn't work out."

"I think he was born angry," I said.

"People shouldn't talk about things they know nothing about," said Grandpa. "Of course, you could castrate the devil, but Kalle doesn't want to. Imagine if that was done to people who were angry… no thank you."

He grimaced, looked at his work one last time, wiped his head with a handkerchief and put on his hat.

"Now we can start work on the hut, boys."

As we went, we heard Black Demon hitting his hooves against the mended walls.

Like a heart beating.

Thump! Thump! Thump!

When twilight fell we'd finished the frame of the hut. It was in the best place, in a crack in the rocks with a view of the evening sky parading its colours in the fjord. A breeze blew through the tarpaulin we used instead of the roof we hadn't had time to make.

Percy had carried down two kapok mattresses. I took pillows, blankets, a torch and a pile of comics.

"Are you really planning on sleeping here tonight?" asked Grandpa. "The hut isn't even half-finished. It's just three walls and a big hole."

"It's a warm night," said Percy. "And we've got blankets."

"What about Buffalo Bill then?" asked Grandpa.

"Grandpa will have to manage without a bedtime story tonight," I said.

"You might like to hear a poem instead?" asked Percy.

"What sort of poem?" asked Grandpa. *It is most beautiful when the sun goes down?*

"No, this one," said Percy.

Buffalo Bill shat with a blast

The Indians thought a bomb had passed.

The seagulls laughed. And Grandpa did too. It was an unusual laugh. It sounded like a car that had been outside in the cold too long and didn't really want to start.

"Ha ha ha ha hahahaha!"

"I'll be blowed if you aren't as silly as you look, you, Percy," he said.

"I know," he said.

"'Night then," said Grandpa, raising his hat.

"'Night," we said.

He went on his way towards the sunset. He looked like a cowboy from behind.

Night, like Percy said, is blacker on an island. The stars shine more brightly, and the moon is somehow closer to the earth.

It's nice to lie back and see if you can spot any flying saucers. We didn't. But we talked. We talked about how we would add onto our hut, till it grew to a skyscraper in our minds. We discussed which kinds of racing cars we would buy when we grew up. And what Klaus's father would look like when Klaus showed him the beetle Percy had made.

"His face will be as long as a hall rug," I said.

I was quite good at similes.

Then Percy talked about how nice it is on an island – and what a fantastic Grandpa I had.

"He's not at all like you said. He's nice."

"Yeah, I don't know what's happened," I said. "Maybe he's got dementia."

"What's that?" said Percy.

"Calcium in the brain," I said. "Old people get it."

"Not him," said Percy. "He's got flippin' uranium in his brain."

We laughed at that. And that made me think about

79

Pia's laugh. I thought about it whenever someone laughed. It made me go serious again.

"What's the matter?" Percy asked.

"You shouldn't talk so much," I said.

"I wasn't talking any more than I normally do," said Percy.

"Well stop it," I said. "You talked a lot down in the village. Don't do that again. In any case not when there are girls around."

Then Percy looked at me. He saw right into my troubled love life.

"You're in love with that girl in the red jersey, aren't you?" he said.

"Why would I be?" I said.

"Admit it!" he said.

He bent my fingers backwards till they cracked, and I got tears in my eyes.

"Yeah – yes – I am – Let go!" I said.

"I knew it," he said, and let go.

"Confessing under torture doesn't count," I said, blowing on my hand. "It's in the Geneva Convention. Besides, it's mostly the way she laughs."

"I was in love with a girl who was cross-eyed," said Percy. "She lived in the same apartment block as me. After a while I went cross-eyed too, out of love, till I got a sore head and Mum took me to a doctor. But whatever I did the girl took no notice. And in the end it passed. It will pass for you too."

"Maybe," I said. "But I don't think so. But now you'll have to keep your mouth shut, because I'm going to learn some funny stories."

I took out *The Best Stories*, turned on the torch and turned to *Humour in Uniform*. I read it.

I just laughed quietly to myself, like Dad did when he thought of a word for his crossword.

"Read it out loud," said Percy.

I read the one about a sergeant.

"Was that funny?" I asked.

"Not really," he said. "Read another one."

So I read one about a captain, then one about a general. I carried on till Percy went to sleep. I turned off the torch. A thousand million stars were blinking at each other above my head. Tomorrow I'd hear Pia's laugh.

But what did I know?

CHAPTER TEN

Love, nettles and vinegar

We were experts at kick-the-can. We played it every summer at the abandoned section beside Odlins'. There were plenty of hiding places. Further down were rushes where you could put the ball we used instead of a can. There were leeches down there.

I'd brushed my teeth, washed my hair and was wearing my yellow fleece jersey and blue shorts. I looked as smart as the Swedish flag. I said to Percy that he didn't need to worry.

"Just try not to be seen," I said.

"I'll do my best," said Percy.

But when we arrived Percy was the only thing anybody looked at. There was Ulf E, Pia, Marianne, Birgitta, Klaus, Benke, Kicki, Bo-Sture and Leif and his little sister, all looking at Percy as if he was the Phantom, the Holy Spirit and Einstein, all in one.

Klaus had just told them what Percy had done.

"How on earth did you think of it?" asked Pia, her eyes glowing.

"Think of what?" said Percy.

"The idea of making up your own beetle," said Birgitta.

"That was really smart," said Benke.

"It was nothing," said Percy. "By the way, what did your Dad say, Klaus?"

"Say?" said Klaus. "He almost couldn't talk. He ran off to get a pile of books and looked and looked. 'Not here either,' he kept saying. Then he rushed off and rang some experts. Tomorrow he's taking the boat to town to show them the beetle. And he gave me twenty-five kronor! Here – you should have them. It's only fair."

Klaus took the notes from his pocket and held them out to Percy.

"Keep them," said Percy. "I wasn't doing it for the money."

Then everyone looked at him as if he was Jesus Christ as well. They even started to introduce them-selves. They were a hair's breadth away from taking him by the hand.

"Nice to see you again," said Pia, fluttering her eye-lashes at him.

I couldn't stand any more of this misery.

"Let's get the game started, for crissakes!" I said.

So we did. Leif got to stand down, like he always did. He was the only one who couldn't work out how to avoid it. He stood with his eyes closed, counting to a hundred, with his little sister in his arms and his foot on the ball, while the rest of us raced off and hid.

I didn't see where Percy went, because I didn't let Pia out of my sight. And when Leif shouted: "One hundred!" I sneaked in behind the same rock as her.

"Fancy you being here!" I said. "What a great hiding place."

"Keep your mouth shut," she said.

Leif found Birgitta who always changed her mind and wanted to change her hiding place, and Ulf E who sneezed when a mosquito went up his nose.

"Ulf E and Birgitta to the can!" shouted Leif.

But after a while the Holy Spirit rushed out and kicked the ball so that it bounced down the hill – then the prisoners were free and Leif had to start again from the beginning. The same thing happened again and again, because Leif had to carry his little sister around, so he hardly ever got to the ball in time.

The whole time I was hiding behind the same stone as Pia.

"Stop hiding with me!" she hissed.

"How should I know that you were here?" I said.

"Don't do it again anyhow," she said.

But I did it again. I couldn't help it. I was drawn there by gravity, the earth's magnetic field and whatever other forces exist. I splashed myself down in a ditch behind the long drop where she'd disappeared.

Unfortunately I went straight into a patch of stinging nettles. A big patch. The nettles were so high they reached up to your elbows.

I shrieked as quietly as I could.

My thighs and left arm were on fire.

"What do you think you're doing?" she asked.

"I've been bliddy stung!" I said.

"I said you should stop hanging around me," she said.

She smiled at my grimacing face. It looked like she was going to laugh, so I decided to use the moment.

"Do you want to hear a funny story?" I asked.

"No thank you," she said.

"Why not?"

"Because your stories aren't funny."

"But this one is," I said.

So I started to tell her the story about the corporal. But Pia just sighed and yawned. It's not easy to be funny.

"Want to hear another?" I asked.

"Don't you understand anything?" she said.

"No," I said.

So I tickled her under the arms instead. That was stupid. But I couldn't stop myself. I had been longing to hear her hoarse laugh so badly that I couldn't go home until I did.

But when she laughed, it wasn't right. It didn't sound like she was happy.

And on top of that of course we got found straight away.

"Pia and Ulf to the can!" shouted Leif.

"This is all your fault!" shouted Pia, dragging herself free from my arms. "Everybody come here!"

Everybody came. Percy came with straw in his hair and a rip in his jersey, looking happy. Pia was so angry that the whole game had to stop. She pointed at me and then stamped her foot so that there was almost an earthquake.

"I will never, ever play again, if he plays," she cried. "He's an idiot!"

"He's just in love," said Percy.

"You shut your mouth," I said. "All I did was tell a joke."

"I could've died of boredom," said Pia.

Then Percy told one of the stories I'd read to him the night before. It was one of the worst ones, about a general who was going to throw a hand grenade. And

Pia laughed her hoarse laugh so hard that the nettle rash flamed like a thousand burning hot needles in my thighs.

"Here's your chance," whispered Percy. "Tell the one about the colonel now."

So I did.

"There was once a colonel who stood in front of his mother," I began.

But when the story was finished Pia hadn't laughed a bit. Klaus laughed. And Benke and Birgitta did too. But Pia just looked at Percy the whole time and smiled, shrugging her shoulders.

"Don't you think they're boring?" she said to him. "Will you come swimming in the harbour with me tomorrow?"

She did say 'you' which could have meant both of us. But she was looking at Percy when she said it.

"Yes, we will," he said.

"I don't think so," I said. "We're leaving now."

"Forget about her," said Percy when we got home. "She doesn't have a sense of humour. Not when it comes to uniforms anyhow."

We were sitting in the hammock, rocking backwards and forwards to calm ourselves down. Grandpa was fixing a gutter. My brother was holding the ladder.

"She should have one," I said. "Because her father is an airline pilot. Why did you have to play the fool in front of her? I told you not to."

"I didn't," said Percy.

"Yes you did!"

"Cripes, I don't even think she's cute. Do you know what she reminds me of? A Pekinese. Yap yap yap!"

He barked and waved his ears.

So I boxed him in the stomach.

"Don't talk about her like that," I said.

I was about to hit him one more time, when he grabbed my arm where it still hurt from the nettle rash. I wailed so much that Grandpa swayed on the ladder.

"What are you two up to?" he shouted.

He came down from the ladder spitting out small nails.

"He got stung by nettles," said Percy.

"And is that anything to shout about?" said Grandpa. "Once I burned half my bum on a boiler. I couldn't sit down for a month. But I didn't go round crying about it."

He lifted me up and carried me over his shoulder to the fixed-up lion chair. Then he got some cotton and a mug of vinegar.

"Will it sting?" I asked.

"It'll sting, but it helps," said Grandpa.

He rubbed the angry rash with vinegar.

It stung so much it gave me goosebumps and brought tears to my eyes. But I didn't complain. I bit my cheek instead.

"How could you get stung so badly?" Grandpa asked.

"Hasn't Grandpa ever been in love?" asked Percy.

"What did you say, boy?"

He turned his sharp blue eyes to my friend.

"Hasn't Grandpa ever been really, truly in love?" repeated Percy.

Grandpa looked over at Grandma who was sitting in a chair smoking, beautiful as always in a grey cardigan and gold earrings.

"I still am," he said quietly.

When he walked past Grandma to pour out the vinegar he tried to stroke her cheek with his hand. She twisted away from him.

"Stop your silliness," she said.

Grandpa went on without a word. Percy and I did too.

We found Grandpa standing by the biggest stone – black as coal and round as a gravestone – in the middle of the strawberry patch. It was as if all his anger and disappointment had been sucked into that stone, making it heavier and blacker, year after year. Grandpa rested his head against it and swore.

"I hate this devil stone!" he growled. "Why did it come here?"

"God must have thrown it there," I said.

Grandpa looked at me with red-rimmed eyes. At first it seemed he didn't recognise me. He put his hand out as if to stroke my hair, but he pulled it back again.

"Maybe that's it, Ulf," he said. "But it's a cursed stone, whichever way you look at it."

"Would Grandpa like me to read a little *Buffalo Bill?*" Percy asked.

"No, go inside for God's sake. I just want a moment by myself."

We left him by the stone.

"Why did you say that the stone comes from God?" asked Percy.

"Come on, let's have a look in the Bible," I said.

CHAPTER ELEVEN

We study the Bible

We were in the back cabin, where Mum and Dad slept. The big family Bible lived there, beneath the chandelier on the round table. It was so heavy that I used it to train my arm muscles. I wanted to look like Cain on page 7. Or like Samson when he tore off a town gate on page 335. I wanted to have big and bulging muscles.

Grandma and Grandpa's Bible was full of pictures by someone called Doré. Right in the beginning there were pictures of *The creation of woman,* which showed Eve climbing out of a bush. She was newly-made, and was on her way to meet Adam. This was before clothes, so she was a nudist. You could see the breasts clearly but a branch happened to hide the lower part.

On page 1051 was the most terrible picture I've ever seen: *The dried-up bones come to life.* There were a whole lot of skeletons putting on their dead skulls. It gave me nightmares.

I wanted to show it to Percy.

But first I put the Bible on the floor and turned to page 287.

We lay on our stomachs so we could look closely.

"You can see here how God throws stones," I said.

The Lord allows stones to rain down on the Amorites, was the name of the picture.

We saw big, deadly hunks of stone raining down from heaven, right on the heads of the Amorites, who were trying to escape on their camels.

"Why is God throwing stones at them?" wondered Percy.

"I haven't a clue," I said. "They were probably naughty – so he got angry."

Percy stroked a fallen camel with his finger.

"It's not right," he said. "It's okay that he got angry at these guys, but what had the camels done to anybody?"

"I don't know," I said. "They probably got caught at the same time. God is a bit like Grandpa. He gets angry easily."

When Grandma came into the room and saw us lying on the floor reading the Bible, she held her hands over her stomach and smiled as if she'd just witnessed a miracle. She was a bit religious.

"How nice that you're studying the Bible," she said.

"We're just looking at it," I said.

"Then I won't disturb you," said Grandma.

When we'd finished looking at the cursed stones, Percy found another picture where God was angry and let rain pour down till the whole earth drowned in a flood of sin. We looked at the animal mothers, fighting to get their babies up onto a cliff.

"Best I learn to swim," said Percy.

"Yeah, in case God gets angry again."

"I was thinking about whether we should swim in the harbour tomorrow."

"Can't we skip it?"

"Nah, I want to have a proper summer holiday on an island. And I've had a bet with Dad that I'll learn to swim twenty metres while I'm here. I'm going to do it. Who taught you to swim?"

"Her name is Britta Low," I said. "She was about fourteen, and I was five. She got money from Mum and Dad to teach me. But she doesn't live here any more."

"Then you'll have to teach me."

I sighed. I sighed because it made me think of Pia.

I didn't want Percy to meet her again.

"How much will you give me?" I asked.

Percy turned his eyes from side to side as if he was counting in his head.

"I'm just joking," I said. "Crawl over to the sofa and lie on your stomach."

I figured that at least he couldn't learn how to swim in a single evening. No one could, so there was nothing to worry about. I showed him how to move his arms first, and then his legs. Then I let him swim the whole way from the sofa bed to the chest of drawers. And then he swam around the round table and over to the painting of the white-powdered ladies.

"One, two, three. One, two, three," I counted.

Percy was an ace at swimming on dry land.

"Thundering snakes," he said, "this is going really well. It's a piece of cake. Let's go and bang a few more planks on the hut."

When he stood up his stomach was covered in dust.

"Okay," I said. "But first I'm going to drown *The Best Stories*. I'm never going to read that magazine ever again!"

We tied the whole pile of magazines to a big stone. Then we rowed out and sank them right in the middle of the fjord.

That's what happens if you try to trick blood brothers, I thought to myself.

That evening Percy read a new chapter out of *Buffalo Bill* to Grandpa and me. Grandpa lay on his sofa and I sat in the chair beside the desk. Percy sat at Grandpa's feet.

He read about how Buffalo Bill had to look after his family at the age of eleven, because his father had died. Then Bill rode off to have dangerous adventures with animals and soldiers.

"He had guts, that's for sure," said Grandpa.

"So do you," said Percy.

"Yes, I do," said Grandpa. "Keep reading."

So Percy did.

I wore out three pairs of moccasins on that journey and I learned the good lesson that thicker soles make it easier to walk on hard ground, he read.

Just when Buffalo Bill was about to seek shelter from a desert storm in a cave full of old human bones, Grandpa went to sleep.

We heard him snoring almost the whole way to the hut. It was really nice there now. It only had three walls but we could imagine the rest of it. We crept under our covers.

"What other things did you do when you were little?" asked Percy.

"I can't remember much. I was just a little kid," I said. "I ate ants. Me and my friends made a raft out of plastic flagons and bits of wood. I made a bow and arrow and shot my brother in the bum."

Percy looked as if he was memorising everything.

"I'll do all that too," he said.

"Nah, leave it alone," I said.

We lay there quietly and saw a big rusty ship go past with its lights on and its portholes glowing. It was like a real ghost ship. It steered towards the blinking lighthouse and blew its horn, as hoarse as Pia's laugh.

"Tomorrow we'll go swimming," said Percy.

Then we went to sleep.

CHAPTER TWELVE

Percy shoots a bull's-eye and almost swims properly

"I'm going to scalp you, you stupid pig-eyed little son of a creep!"

I woke to my brother's voice. He was shouting wildly from the lawn beside the house. Next door the school teacher was practising a funeral hymn. When I had un-hitched myself from my bedclothes and reached the house, I saw Jan running after Percy. He was almost hopping, gasping for breath. Percy was carrying an arrow in his hand.

My brother soon caught up with him.

"What's he done?" I called.

"I was just standing there taking a pee and he shot me in the bum," said my brother.

"It was probably a mistake," I said.

"I don't think so," my brother said and he broke the arrow in two. "Don't do it again," he said to Percy. "If you do I'll prick you a thousand times in the bum with a red-hot fork. Do you understand?"

"Yes," said Percy.

Jan drew breath and went away.

"Enjoying yourself?" I said.

"I've eaten ants as well, this morning," said Percy. "And straightened half a bucket of nails. Snakes alive, you've been asleep for hours."

He was very efficient, Percy.

"Yeah, but can we take things a bit more quietly?" I said. "I did that a lot when I was little. I took things quietly. And I skipped stones."

"What – you jumped over stones?"

"You have no idea, do you," I said.

So I took him down to the beach. I showed him how to choose stones that were thin and flat. Not too heavy. But not too light either because then the wind could catch them.

"You hold them between your thumb and finger like this. And then you throw them so they spin like flying saucers over the water."

I found a good stone and showed him. It flew away just like it should. When it hit the water, it skipped like a water flea over the surface.

"Eight jumps," I said proudly. "You won't beat that for a while."

He did it in half an hour.

"Now it would be nice if we could both jump in too," said Percy.

You can find anything you'll ever need in the workshop. We found the inner tube of a car tyre and filled it with air. Then we carried it down to the harbour, where the water was calm. We were there so early that I thought we would have it to ourselves.

"If Pia turns up, don't think about being funny," I said.

Percy's head nodded above the surface of the water.

He had jumped in already, because he was so keen to learn to swim. He stood on the bottom with the car tyre in front of his nose. Two duck feathers, now attached to a band on his head, fluttered in the morning breeze. He had the cork belt around his stomach.

"It's cold," he muttered.

"You'll get used to it," I promised. "We'll start with kicking. Keep your hands in front of you on the tyre. And kick with your legs like you did yesterday – remember?"

"Of course I can. I don't have calcium in the brain," he said.

"Off you go then," I said.

I stood on the jetty and called out as if I was an experienced swimming instructor.

"Out with your legs now, properly. And together again!" I called. "You're not on the floor now. That's the story!"

He swam away like a giant frog, with powerful leg strokes and a steady grip on the tyre. He was really good. I'd learned to swim when I was five years old. When I was six, I got my swimming medallion. I had always believed I was a wonder child.

"That's good, keep it up!" I called. "Think about God."

He passed the motor boat buoys and the seagulls shrieked as if he was swimming in the Swedish Masters. I was just about to pull off my trousers and jump in after him when I saw Pia.

She was on her way down the hill. She was wearing a yellow dress with a red belt around her middle and she was carrying a swimming towel in her hand. The wind made the dress flap against her legs. And she was walking in a special, sort of light and dancing way, which made her hair swing.

I pulled in my tummy.

"Hello," I said, when she came closer.

"Are you here already?" she said.

"Yes," I said.

"You're not telling funny stories today?" she said.

"No-o," I said. "I drowned them."

Then I talked quite a lot. I told her my brother had

been shot with an arrow in the bum that morning. And that she had a really nice dress. And that Grandpa had sworn at a big stone for a whole hour yesterday. I talked just for the pleasure of seeing her listen. And so she wouldn't ask about Percy.

"What have you done with Percy then?" she asked, when I paused for breath.

"I'm teaching him to swim," I said. "He can't even do that."

She perused the water.

"Where is he?"

I turned around and looked.

I saw the waves glittering in the sun, clucking and splashing against the boats in the harbour. I saw a pair of gulls dive and come up again. But where was Percy? At last I caught a glimpse of him. He was at the entrance to the harbour. A couple of duck feathers were sticking up, on their way out to the fjord where the waves were high.

"Cripes!" I said. "I forgot to watch him."

"Where is he?" said Pia.

"He's on his way to Russia," I said.

I ran as fast as I could. I jumped over the hedge with the leeches. And I raced past the row of boats.

"I'm coming, wait for me!" I shouted.

On the way to the pier I grabbed a boat hook hanging off a boathouse. At the end of the jetty there was a slippery wooden beam. I stood on the end of it and reached out as far as I could to grab hold of the cork belt and pull in Percy – who was swimming without turning his head. But however hard I tried, I couldn't reach him. He was gliding out into the line of the ferries with the car tyre in front of him.

"Keep calm, I'll get you," I called.

"How am I doing?" he called back.

Then he was swept off by a big, grey wave.

It took a while before I got hold of a dinghy with oars in it, so I could row out after him. He had already drifted towards the middle of the fjord. A big Russian ship with a rusty hull was heading straight towards him.

"Look out!" I shrieked.

But how could he hear me?

The ship held its course. Then I couldn't see the head with the duck feathers any more – until the ship went past.

I finally reached Percy, but he couldn't get himself up into the dinghy and I had to tow him back to the harbour. Klaus had arrived and he stood beside Pia. Together we hauled Percy onto the jetty, where he lay gasping like a flounder on dry land.

"What were you doing out there?" I said.

"I couldn't turn around with that car tyre in front of me," he said. "What did you think of my kicking?"

"Perfect," I said.

"Good," he said, spitting out water. "But next time we won't train for such a long time."

His lips were blue and his teeth chattered.

"You're supposed to be his friend," said Pia to me. "He could have drowned."

She placed her hand on his brow.

"He's frozen," she said. "We have to get his body temperature up."

Pia sounded like the capable nurse she was going to be. She took out the pink towel that had once made me dizzy with the smell of her and placed it over Percy. She rubbed his arms and chest.

"You'll soon warm up," she said.

"That's a bit unnecessary," I said.

She looked at me as if I was a cold-blooded murderer.

"You can't talk," she said. "You almost killed him."

"At least I pulled him back to land," I said.

Then Percy threw off the towel.

"Stop your bickering," he said. "I'm alive. Let's race home and play something fun. Coming, Klaus?"

"Course I am," said Klaus.

Pia folded up her towel as if it was a treasure.

"Are you coming to the dance on Saturday?" she asked Percy.

"We'll see," said Happy Cloud.

We didn't get to play any games that day.

First we wanted to show Klaus our hut. Grandpa was already there. He said he'd had a second to spare, so he was putting in a window. He'd already sawn a hole and cut a piece of glass with a diamond cutter.

"What good timing," he said. "Step to it and give me a hand!"

So we did. We helped put the window together and hang it up. The view was like a picture with the fjord shining in the midday sun, and two fishing boats.

"Soon you'll be able to call it a house," said Grandpa.

"When it's finished we can buy a chandelier and a radio gramophone," said Percy.

"And a Persian rug," I said.

Grandpa looked at the gold watch which hung from a chain in his waistcoat.

"Well I never – almost lunchtime."

He grunted happily and put on his hat. Then suddenly he froze.

"What in the name of brimstone!" he shouted.

He was looking at a pair of crows circling the cherry tree. He threw a stone at the birds. But the crows just laughed at him high in the sky.

That didn't calm him down at all.

"Vermin! If I didn't see so badly I'd shoot you," he shouted.

The crows flew off to the school teacher's garden.

"He can have them," chuckled Grandpa. "He coughs so much it disturbs my snoring. So boys – would you like to learn how to shoot?"

"Yeah, that would come in handy," said Percy.

"I have to go home for lunch," said Klaus.

"Shame," I said. "When does your Dad come home?"

"On Saturday," said Klaus.

And off he went. Percy, Grandpa and me went home to the wardrobe where we took the cabin-rifle from behind Grandma's winter coat. It was a proper gun – it took real bullets. Grandpa handed it to me. Then he set up empty paint tins on the stones beside the potato patch.

"Try to hit the tins," he said. "Pretend they are crows or squirrels or some other pest."

"You can't shoot squirrels," said Percy.

"And why not?" shouted Grandpa. "They ruin my strawberries. They don't even eat them – they just take a bite out of every berry."

He showed us how to load and aim. But I already knew how, because my brother and I had practised in secret. Grandpa put in the first bullet.

"Percy can go first because he's the guest," he said.

Percy hit a tin of Beckers red paint with his first shot.

"Beginner's luck," I said.

While we practised, Grandpa told us how Buffalo Bill had shot a record number of buffalo when the railway line was being laid across America.

"You can't call a man who shoots innocent animals a hero," said Percy, shooting down another paint tin.

"You're a pain in the butt for talking back," said Grandpa. "Billy was a brave man. Enough said."

We shot more holes in the tins. Then Mum came out with a smoking frying pan in her hand. When she saw me lift the rifle, she dropped the frying pan with the chops in it, and rushed towards us. I didn't know she was so good at running.

"Ulf! Put that thing down immediately!" she yelled. "What were you thinking Grandpa – letting children use live ammunition! I knew you were half crazy, but I didn't know you were an irresponsible dolt!"

"Calm down, Ebba," Grandpa said.

"No I will not calm down," she screamed. "I cook your dinner, wash your underwear and iron your shirts. And what do you do? You put the children's lives in danger. I'm sick of it. I'm going home! Kurt can do what he likes. But I'm taking the children with me!"

She rushed off to the house with me and Percy in tow.

"There there, little one," called Grandpa. "At least let me keep Percy for a bit. I've started to like him."

"No! You are not suitable company!"

Inside, she started hurling things into the big trunk – socks, dresses, the kitchen mixer, all in together. Then she put on her town hat and her sunglasses.

"But dear, sweet Ebba," said Grandpa.

"No," she said and sat down on the trunk, shaking.

After a while Dad put away the crossword and came and sat down beside her. Tears ran from the bottom edge of her sunglasses.

"Little one," said Dad.

"I am not little," she said.

"What happened?" asked Dad.

"If you looked up from your crossword you would know," said Mum. "And by the way it is Swiss roll!"

"What is?" asked Dad.

"The word you can't get in your crossword. The jammed cylinder. Five plus four," said Mum.

I saw how angry Mum looked, and how Dad was hurt. Percy and I stood by the Bible and didn't know what to do. Then we heard the thundering of hooves. We opened the door. A black horse was galloping at full speed over the vegetable patch. It shook its head. It bared its teeth and neighed as it rushed towards freedom.

"Black Demon!" Mum said. "He's kicked himself loose again. I hope they never catch him." She sounded as if she was happy for Black Demon.

"I hope so too," said Percy.

But then Black Demon saw the path and he headed straight towards our house. He reared up in front of the door, pawing his front legs in the air. Then he carried on towards the school teacher's garden.

Some men from the village came running up next. Mum stepped outside.

"That way," she said, pointing in the wrong direction.

"Why did you say that?" Dad asked when the men had disappeared in the direction she'd shown.

"Why shouldn't he have a moment of freedom?" said Mum. "All of us should."

"You're right," said Grandpa. "As you are in most things. I am so sorry."

Mum sighed, picked up the frying pan and the chops, and went and unpacked her things.

"What was all that about?" Dad asked me. "Had you done something?"

"No, not especially," said Percy.

"Because you know, Ulf," Dad said, "if there is something, you can always come to me and talk about it."

"Yes," I said.

He patted me on the shoulder, went into the back cabin and picked himself out a detective novel.

CHAPTER THIRTEEN

Percy dances and gets punched — twice

On Saturday evenings, there was always a dance on the island. A lamp was lit by the outdoor pavilion. Sometimes an orchestra came from town. Otherwise they played a gramophone. The music bounced towards the arch of the sky and made the mosquitoes and sandflies and people dance.

But we didn't dance. We were too young and too old to dance.

We got in through a hole in the fence out back. Sometimes we bought a sausage in a bun and chocolate milk from Margareta in the kiosk. Sometimes we smoked a cigarette behind a bush. But most times, we just watched.

We looked to see who was kissing who, and who disappeared into the woods when they thought no one was looking.

"Look at those two!"

"Can you see where he's put his hand?"

We took bets on who we thought would get most drunk and we waited to see if anyone would get into a fight. Once we threw uncooked peas over the dance floor.

But we never danced. It was an unwritten law. If it was a really good orchestra we might tap the beat a little with one foot. We talked and we looked. That was enough.

Today we were talking about Black Demon. He had been caught after two days of freedom. You could see where branches had scratched his skin. Five strong men were needed to hold him. Black Demon bit one and kicked another in the leg.

"They're saying that they might have to put him down," Marianne said.

"They can't just kill him," said Pia.

"They can do whatever they like," said Leif, who was carrying his little sister on his shoulders.

"He'll have to be tied up in the stable now," I said.

We stood and thought about the poor crazy horse that had to be tied up in the middle of summer.

"He should be set free," said Percy.

"I think so too," said Pia.

Then we didn't know what to say next. Percy slapped

a mosquito. Leif drank the dregs of a bottle of beer he'd found. Marianne hummed the song that was playing.

"Is this what you do every summer?" said Percy. "Just stand here and watch?"

"Yes," I said. "See that man there? He usually gets angry when he's drunk."

"What's fun about that? Don't you ever dance?" asked Percy.

"What do you think?" I giggled.

"Yeah, well I'm going to," he said.

He left before I could tell him not to. He asked an older woman in her thirties, who was standing by the fence looking sad. She was wearing a short skirt, a leather jacket and sunglasses, even though the sun had gone down a long time ago. She spat out her chewing gum and followed him onto the dance floor.

"I wonder what he's going to do," said Benke.

"Come on, lets watch," said Leif.

We thought Percy would do something really clever and cool. Maybe he would put out his leg so that the woman fell over and her skirt would fly up. We climbed up on the rail and looked, but when we caught sight of Percy, he was just dancing, normal as anything. He held one hand on the woman's back and the other was out straight. His legs went apart and then together, as if he was swimming breaststroke.

Percy was good at dancing with people who were taller than him. He'd been practising with his mother since he learned to walk.

"Why is nothing happening?" Leif asked.

The song finished and Percy bowed politely to the woman, who looked happier now.

"What the hell was that?" giggled Benke.

"Yeah, he just danced!" I said.

I wanted Percy to make a fool of himself – to pay for having been under Pia's pink bathing towel.

When he came back we were all quiet.

Everyone but Pia.

"I want to dance too," she said.

She took Percy's hand and pulled him towards the dance floor. At first he looked doubtful. But then he shrugged his shoulders in my direction. He took her by the waist and twirled away among the others.

I didn't want to watch, but I couldn't help it.

I saw she'd put one hand on Percy's shoulder. She laughed in his ear and pressed tightly against him, because it was a slow song. But the moment she laughed was the worst of all.

I got tears in my eyes.

Then Klaus came along.

"Well, what did your father say?" I asked. "Was he cross? Did they find out the beetle was home-made?"

"Of course they did. They were experts," said Klaus. "They laughed at Dad because he'd been tricked by a kid. They laughed so hard that Dad lost interest in biology altogether, and in botany too. He said to me, 'You've helped me understand what snobs those scientists are. Never show me another beetle again. Nor a flower, nor a butterfly.' Then he gave me another twenty kronor. Isn't that great! Now maybe I won't have to do something useful every summer. Are you listening, Ulf?"

"Sure," I said.

But I wasn't. I was watching the two P's, Percy and Pia. Plunder and Pest. Pottie and Piss!

Klaus followed my eyes and saw how they were twirling around, like a marvellous carousel.

"Are they dancing?" he said, sounding as if he was going to be sick.

"Come on," he said, "let's go and have a ciggy. My shout. You look like you need one."

When the song finished after three cigarettes and five mosquito bites we went back. Percy bowed to Pia and then he winked at me. Pia had red cheeks.

"Wow, that was fantastic," she said.

"Aw, perhaps it's worth giving it a go," said Benke. "What do you say, Ulf?"

"Shut your mouth," I said.

"What will you do then?" said Percy.

"If you come with me I'll tell you," I said.

We went behind the dance floor where a few couples were hugging.

"Okay, what do you want to say?" said Percy.

"This," I said.

I hit Percy. I did it because Pia had laughed in his ear. I boxed him hard in the stomach. After that we wrestled for a while. Percy was overpowered and I got him onto his back.

"I wish you'd never come!" I puffed. "I wish we'd never become blood brothers!"

Percy lay completely still and stared at me.

"What's the matter with you?" he said.

"Why did you have to dance with her?" I said.

"Listen," he said, pushing me away. "You never say no when a girl asks you for a dance. That's just how it is. We'll go back to the others now."

So we did.

But when we got back, only Pia and Klaus were left. Marianne was dancing with Ulf E. Benke was dancing with Birgitta. And Leif had his little sister in his arms.

"Do you want another dance, Percy?" Pia asked.

"Sorry," he said. "Ulf hits so hard that I'm not really in form."

"Then it's best that we go home," I said.

We went home by the inland route. A sorrowful waltz could be heard from the pavilion, matching our feelings perfectly. The fir trees were blacker than before. The birds were quiet. And in the sky, there were no stars. I put my hands in my pockets, so they wouldn't do anything stupid.

"I'm sorry I hit you," I said. "And I didn't mean that about not being blood brothers."

"You don't have to worry about that," said Percy.

"I don't know why I'm like this. I wish I could just forget her."

"Can't you do that then?"

"Nah… You should have come here last year instead. Or next year."

"This year's good. This is the best summer I've ever had. And it's not finished yet."

"Being in love is like being sick," I said.

We carried on talking about love for a while; that it made you do things that you'd never normally do. And say things you didn't mean. It made you happy and sad at the same time.

"She doesn't care about me," I said.

"She can't do that forever," said Percy. "Because you're the best there is!"

"I know," I said. "But whatever happens you should ignore her!"

Then I hit Percy again. On his lip this time. I couldn't understand how my hand could just jump up out of my pocket without me knowing.

He licked away the blood.

"Sorry again," I said. "You can hit me back if you want."

"Just for the sake of it then," he said, and hit me on the nose.

Then we carried on in silence. He licked his lip. And I held a handkerchief under my nose.

When we got home Grandpa was gazing out over the fjord.

"Are you enjoying the view, Grandpa?" I asked.

"Not at all," he said. "I'm just thinking about whether I should plant another cherry tree – beside that bugger of a stone."

Then he noticed Percy's swollen lip and my nose.

"Have you been fighting, boys?"

"Just for fun," Percy said.

"Not," I said. "Percy is so flippin' stupid."

I knew I was being unfair. Percy looked down at the ground. And that made me even more angry.

"I'm not going to talk to him ever again!" I said.

"Don't be an idiot, Ulf," said Grandpa. "With a real

friend you should fall out sometimes and have a fight now and again. That's how it is."

"You can fight with your old stones," I said. "Or ask your friend here to read you *Buffalo Bill*."

I turned my back and walked away. I thought that Grandpa would be angry. But then I turned round and saw him smiling.

"That's good," he said. "You got that temperament from me. But then your name is Gottfrid, just like mine."

"That's your fault," I said. Then I went and lay down in the draughty hut. After a while Percy came too. He brushed his teeth and put on the tracksuit he used as pyjamas.

"Shall we build a raft in the morning?" he said. "Made out of plastic bottles and old planks?"

I pretended I couldn't hear him.

"Then maybe you'd forget to be so cross all the time," he said.

I picked my nails.

"Won't you answer?"

I burrowed my head into the pillow.

"Forget it. It's nice to have a bit of quiet. But you can forget about thinking that you can stop being friends with me. Go'night, Gottfrid!"

Percy went to sleep straight away. I lay there and saw the clouds gather like big black stones on the horizon.

After a while I got up. At first I thought that I needed to pee. But then I noticed that I was on my way to the village.

I climbed up a maple tree on Pia's section and sat on a branch. I looked in through her window with Grandpa's binoculars.

Pia lay in bed reading. She was wearing a white night-dress with blue flowers on it. On the chest of drawers beside her was a travelling gramophone made of plastic. Every now and then she twisted a piece of her hair, as if she was thinking. Elvis Presley sang to me through a gap in the window.

Are you lonesome tonight? he crooned.

Yes, I was. I'd never been so lonesome.

Just me and a swarm of mosquitoes.

"Dear God, let her get up and smile at me," I asked. "Let her wave me into her room and tell me I'm the one she likes and then kiss me. Make a miracle! Is it too much to ask?"

What was God's answer to that?

It started raining. And when Elvis had finished his song, Pia turned off the light. I sat there for an hour and let God pour water on me.

I was getting crosser and crosser.

CHAPTER FOURTEEN

I hear the music of love

Next day my body was covered in fiery mosquito bites, which I scratched open. On top of that I had a cold. In the morning I worked on a puzzle Mum had brought called *Sky and Sea*.

There were two thousand pieces in different shades of blue.

Percy couldn't bear to watch. He lay on his stomach practising swimming from the dining room to the back cabin, then into the kitchen where Mum gave him a piece of anchovy while she was making lunch. Percy pretended he was a seal.

"Will you be finished soon?" he called.

"Nah," I said.

I didn't want to finish. I wanted to drown my feelings in all that blue. But it wasn't so easy.

It was as if I was divided into two. One Ulf wanted

to meet Pia more than anything in the whole world. And the other one never wanted to see her again.

"What are you thinking about?" asked Percy.

"Nothing special," I said.

"You're thinking about Pia," he said.

"I'm thinking about doing the same as Grandpa."

"How's that?" said Percy.

"Persevere," I said. "Grandma said she married Grandpa because he never gave up. That might work."

"I don't think so," said Percy. "How long are you here for?"

"A few more weeks."

"You'll hardly have time," he said. "It can take years."

"What shall I do then?"

"I'll talk to her," said Percy. "She listens to me, as you might have noticed."

"But what will you say to her?"

"It'll come," he said. "Don't forget there's uranium in my brain."

He smiled so convincingly that I had to smile back.

"Shall we build that raft now?" I said.

"Nah, let's go swimming," he said.

But first we had to eat. Then we had to wait an hour or we'd get cramp and die, Dad said. So we nailed up the last wall in the hut instead.

"This is the most beautiful hut I've ever built," I said.

"Yes," said Percy. "But let's go swimming now. Last one in is a scaredy pants!"

I got to be the scaredy pants. When I dived in, Percy was already standing on the sludgy bottom with his cork belt around his waist.

"Look," he said.

He swam three perfect swimming strokes without touching the bottom.

"What do you say now then?" he said proudly, spitting out water.

"Impossible, yet true," I said.

"Now I'll treat you to tiger cake," he said. "Because I'll be blowed if I'm not worth it."

"Where will you get one from?" I said.

"I'll make it myself," he said. "Did you like the cake I brought with me?"

"Yeah," I said. "But you said it was from your mother."

"That's just the sort of thing you have to say," said Percy. "I'll take off my cork belt now."

He threw it up onto the jetty. Then he swam underwater till Klaus came and sat on the jetty, splashing his toes in the water.

"Why don't you take your shorts off," said Percy. "Swimming is cool."

"We're going shopping after," I said. "Percy is going to bake a tiger cake."

"Jump in!" said Percy.

Klaus shook his head and looked gloomy.

"Can't," he said. "Dad has decided we should sail around in our boat for a week living off nature. It's to celebrate me tricking science. We're going to learn how to survive."

"On what?" I asked.

"On snakes and berries and things like that," said Klaus. "Dad's waiting in the boat. See you, guys."

"Bye, Klaus," I said. "Hope you survive."

"We'll save you a piece of tiger cake," promised Percy.

After that we went up to the house. Percy got some money from the reserve supply he kept in a sock in his suitcase. Dad looked up from his book.

"And where are you two going?" he asked.

"To the shop. Why's that?" I said.

"I just wanted to know what you're up to," he said. "You might as well buy me a copy of *Across and Down* while you're there."

He gave me ten kronor and told me I could keep the change.

Percy got the things he needed and also a furry fire-engine-red rug for our hut. I bought Dad's magazine and

122

some cheese. As well as that we got two banana ice-creams.

"Mmmm," said Percy. "Soon I'll be able to swim twenty metres."

"Mmmm," I said.

We dawdled our way home. When we drew even with the dance pavilion Pia came cycling towards us with her hair flying, braking right beside us.

"Hi," she said. "That was cool fun yesterday."

"It was OK," I said.

"Tomorrow it's the movies," she said to Percy. "Can't we go to the movies? Ulf can come too. It's a love movie. They're naked in it."

They held movies at the pavilion on Mondays. They put sheets of paper over the windows and put up a white screen. The best thing was that the doorkeepers didn't care about the age limit.

I could see the poster on the fence. It was called: *She danced one summer*. The title was terrifying, and the picture was even worse: a young woman smiling at a young man in an embarrassing, in-love sort of way.

"I have something to say to you first," said Percy.

"What would that be?" said Pia, laughing.

"It's nothing to laugh at, it's about love," said Percy.

"Don't say it," I said.

"Go ahead," said Pia. "I think I feel the same way."

She smiled as idiotically as the woman in the picture.

"Ulf's in love with you," said Percy. "He's thinking about you all the time. Can't you be together with him?"

"Why should I?" she said.

"Because there isn't anyone better," said Percy. "Believe me. I've been best friends with him for three years now. First I thought he was just a chubby spoilt bloke who wasn't 'specially smart and didn't know much. But then I got to know him. And it turns out that he's the best guy on earth."

"It doesn't matter," she said. "I'm not in love with him."

"You will be," he said.

Then Pia looked at me, and shook her head.

"Sorry Ulf, it won't work," she said. "It's impossible."

"What do you mean impossible?" I said. "How much impossible?"

"Completely impossible," she said. "Like counting the grains of sand in the Sahara, like drinking up the Baltic Sea, like riding Black Demon."

"Black Demon," I said, and then I understood how impossible it was.

She got back on her bicycle. She looked at Percy.

"Why wasn't it you instead?" she said and cycled away.

I took an egg out of Percy's lunchbox and threw it as hard as I could against the woman on the poster.

"Hell-ridden love louse!" I shouted.

"Don't give up," said Percy and he put his arm around my shoulders.

But what did I have to hope for?

When we got home, I snuck down to the big black stone and rested my forehead against it, like Grandpa did when he was sad.

But it didn't help.

I was filled with the weight of the Dark Ages.

Grandpa came over. He took me by the scruff of the neck and pulled me away.

"You shouldn't stand there. What's wrong, Ulf Gottfrid?" he asked.

"Nothing," I said.

Grandpa saw my tears, like a sea of sorrow.

"I think there is," he said in a soft voice that I almost didn't recognise.

"Leave me alone," I said.

"He's unhappy in love," said Percy.

"How long has he been like this?" said Grandpa.

"More than a week," I said.

"Poor thing," said Grandpa.

He told us how he'd met Grandma when she was young. She was living on the island, but she'd come to town on the boat. Back then she had hair that shone as if it had been brushed by the sun. And he fell in love – pang-boom!

"Just like this," said Grandpa, clapping his hands together. "It's never gone away, even though I wished it would many times, because she never got to think about me in the same way. And when I see that devil of a stone I think about it. One day I'm going to lift that stone and throw it to the end of the world."

"Nobody could lift that stone," said Percy. "Not someone fat and old like you, anyway."

"Maybe you're right," said Grandpa.

I rested my head against Grandpa's tummy. I could hear time ticking in there. It was the gold watch. I thought about how much time the minutes take when you're sad. Imagine being unhappy for a whole lifetime!

"What shall I do, Grandpa?" I said.

"Go and get me some milk," he said.

We sat on the veranda steps with a glass of milk each, watching the deep blue sky slowly change to violet. The shadows became longer. The butterflies closed their wings for the night.

"Now we'll go to the workshop," said Grandpa.

We collected a crowbar and then we went to the place where the cliff was steepest down to the fjord. You could see all the way to the horizon. The lighthouse blinked. Sometimes Grandma used to sit there to smoke and enjoy the view.

We sat beside a pair of big stones, listening to the sounds of the evening. A tanker passed with all its lights on. When it disappeared it was dark enough.

"We'll do it now," said Grandpa, standing up.

"What?" I asked.

He didn't answer.

He took the crowbar and drove in the point of it under the biggest stone.

"Grab hold and be quiet!" he said.

We pushed the crowbar with all our might. The ground squeaked. And in the end we got the stone to move, centimetre by centimetre, towards the edge of the cliff. Then it was stuck for a few seconds and seemed to hesitate, as if it was dizzy.

"Now!" shouted Grandpa.

I pushed so hard my eyes were flaming red. And then the stone began to roll, at first slowly and then faster and faster. It bounced down the cliff, ripping up moss and earth, breaking the bushes and undergrowth in its path. It threw sparks and it boomed like thunder. It was like fireworks.

"Do you hear that?" shouted Grandpa. "Can you hear the MUSIC OF LOVE?"

"Yes," I said, even though I didn't understand.

The stone hit the water with a mighty splash.

Then it was quiet again.

"Now we'll go home," said Grandpa. "Well Ulf, do you feel better now?"

"Maybe a little," I said.

Then we went back inside. Grandma was sitting looking at the window. She wiped her nose in a handkerchief.

"What did that achieve?" she said.

Grandpa went into his cabin.

"Go'natt," he said.

"Goodnight," we said.

I went out to the hut. Percy said he would come in a while. It took him at least an hour. But he brought with him a fresh tiger cake and a thermos of hot chocolate. We sat on the red rug and ate and drank while God lit millions of stars. Then we went to bed.

When I closed my eyes I could still hear the thunder of love's music and I could see the sparks being thrown to the sky.

CHAPTER FIFTEEN

I am gloomy but Percy is fine

Percy wasn't there when I woke up next morning.

There was just a mark in the furry rug where he'd been sleeping. I waited a while, in case he'd just got up for a pee.

Then I got up as well.

It was early. The dewdrops were shining in the spider webs like Mum's jewels. Steam was rising from the moss when the sun warmed it.

First I looked in the woods. He wasn't there, or in the woodshed, on the beach or in the workshop. Inside the house everyone was asleep except Grandma. She was looking out over the fog in the fjord, having the first cigarette of the day. She'd opened the window and blew the smoke out through the crack.

"Hello, Grandma," I said.

"You're up early today," she said. "This is my

favourite moment on earth, before the world wakes up. Would you like coffee?"

"Yes, please."

"Then you can grind it while I finish smoking."

Usually I didn't drink coffee, because it contained caffeine which Dad said was a poison. But Grandma didn't care about that. And I thought it tasted good with lots of cream and sugar. Best of all I liked the smell when you ground the brown beans to powder in the coffee grinder.

We made the coffee and went out onto the balcony.

"This is the time I have to myself," said Grandma. "When the air is freshest and nature is most beautiful. Where is your small friend?"

"I don't know," I said.

"Probably went for a walk," said Grandma. "He's like Grandpa – doesn't like to sit still. He's bound to come back soon."

We didn't talk much more. We saw a pair of squirrels in the pine trees, and a crow sitting in the cherry tree pecking holes in the berries. A gull that had eaten blueberries dropped a lilac stain on the outdoor seat that Grandpa had just finished painting.

It felt good to sit and be quiet with Grandma, seeing her smile so there were little laughing lines at the corner of her eyes and hear her laugh at all the mischief caused by nature. Grandpa would have loved to be sitting here instead of me.

Life is not fair, I thought.

"It's not very fair, life," I said.

"Maybe not," said Grandma. "But that probably means something."

Grandma and I sat there till we heard the school teacher cough and spit in the house next door. Then he began to play a funeral hymn on the piano. He clinked the keys so hard that everyone understood it was time to wake up if you were going to get anything done before you were dead. The hens started to cackle, the snails got up speed and Dad came out in his nightshirt and yawned. He asked if I wanted to do morning gymnastics with him.

"No thank you," I said. "I'm going down to the hut."

Dad bounced up and down and waved so that the arms of his nightshirt flapped. If Percy had been there he'd have said that Dad looked like an angel with a flying problem.

But he wasn't there.

He didn't come until an hour later, when Mum had finished laying the breakfast table under the umbrella: butter, herring, meatballs, boiled eggs, beetroot salad, two kinds of bread, cheese, sour milk, coffee and milk. Percy's shorts were ripped at the back. He had a fresh graze on one knee and he seemed irrepressibly pleased.

"Oh boy, I'm so hungry!" he said.

"Where've you been?" I asked. "Did you meet someone?"

"I s'pose you could say so," he said. "Boy, this looks good."

"Who?" I said.

"Can't tell," said Percy.

He started to spread a thick layer of butter on some bread.

"I know," said my brother. "He's been down and kissed Pia on the mouth."

"As if I care!" I said, leaving the table. "Thanks for the food!"

"Won't you have a meatball?" asked Dad.

"No, I'm going to starve to death," I said.

I went into the back cabin and rested my head against the floorboards. I felt seasick.

After a while Percy came.

"Your brother is just teasing you," he said. "Shall we build a carousel? I found a ball-bearing in the workshop. Then we can get all the small kids to pay us."

"Nah," I said. "I'm going out."

Every morning it was the same. When I woke up, Percy had disappeared. And every breakfast he came back with a wide smile and a new wound – a scratch on his cheek, a sprained ankle, a bite in one shoulder. And then a graze on his stomach!

How do you get a graze on your stomach?

Dad wondered about that too. He got a bottle of iodine from the medicine cupboard.

"What on earth have you been doing?" he asked.

"I can't tell you," said Percy.

"Well, I suppose I can't force you to," said Dad. "This is going to hurt."

Dad spread the iodine with a cotton ball. Percy's tummy went golden brown. He bit his teeth together and made a face. I thought about my right eyebrow, the nettle stings and all the pain of love.

"Serves you right," I said, when Dad had gone.

"What do you mean?" said Percy.

"Don't pretend," I said. "It would be better if you packed your little bag and left the island right now!"

"Do you really mean that?" he said.

"Yes," I said.

"No, Ulf," he said. "I won't leave here, not for a while. See this?"

He waved his left thumb at me.

"Yes," I said.

I could see the scar from the knife when we had mixed blood.

"We're blood brothers," he said. "You don't leave each other. But if you want to be alone for a bit, then I think you should go off somewhere."

I put my scarred thumb against his.

"Goodbye," I said.

I thought that I could write a love letter. That's what Dad had done to Mum when they were young. That had gone quite well. So I took my pen and paper and went off to find aloneness.

On the field by the harbour the midsummer pole was still standing. There were competitions there every year: sack races, spoon and potato races. Leif and his little sister were there now. Leif's sister was tottering around with a spoon in her mouth and she fell over the whole time.

"Hello Ulf," said Leif. "I'm training up my little sister for next year. She's going to win a bar of chocolate. Do you want to join us?"

"No, I have to be alone so I can think," I said.

I took the long way round past the house where Grandma was born. It was a little red house with just one room and a kitchen. Grandma had lived there with her parents and five sisters. I thought how strange it was that she'd grown up here, when she seemed so high-born.

I went on to the beacon. It was highest up on a cliff. That would be the best place to think. The beacon looked like a wigwam. Big logs had been raised so they rested against each other. On the top was a barrel of tar you could light if a foreign ship came past.

I sat on a rock and took out my paper and pen.

I wrote:

Dearest Pia! I can't think of anything but you. Therefore I ask you to change your mind and be together with me, even though you don't want to. In a few years' time you will probably get used to it.

Yours in eternity's eternity, Ulf.

Then I tore the letter into a thousand small pieces that I let drift in the wind. They flew towards the post office, the bakery and the cemetery.

My hopelessness snowed down over the whole village.

I waited till Pia had cycled past on her way to the shop. It hurt in my chest. When she was gone, I went home again. The school teacher still sat at his piano.

Open your window. Let a little sunshine in, he sang.

I wrote a message that I passed in to him.

I THINK YOU SHOULD CLOSE YOURS, I wrote.

Then I went looking for Percy. I found him in the workshop, bent over the bench sewing a pair of clasps into the ends of a leather strap.

"Feel better now?" he asked.

"No," I said. "What's that going to be?"

"I'd rather not say," said Percy.

"Has it got something to do with Pia?"

"You might say so. But we won't talk about her."

"No," I said. "I'm glad you didn't leave."

"Yes," said Percy. "Because tomorrow it will be better."

"I doubt it," I said. "Another day, another sorrow."

I don't know where I got that last bit from.

Percy and I went down to the beach and threw stones at old cans. It wasn't much fun. But it still felt good to be together.

That evening we took our places in Grandpa's cabin. I sat at the end of the bed. Grandpa lay on his back. His stomach rose like the Rockies under the cover. Percy sat on a chair and read aloud from *Buffalo Bill*. It was one of the best chapters, the sixth, called 'My adventures as a pony express rider'. It started like this:

I was now fifteen years old and my appetite for adventure grew increasingly strong. In just a few months I had

completely forgotten my suffering in the cabin and my
decision to never more leave for the border country. I was
looking for something new and even more exciting.

Percy read so that I forgot where I was.

He read about how Buffalo Bill rode around in the Rockies. He carried the post he was supposed to deliver in a water-tight bag. He rode over the prairie like lightning. And he was constantly chased by Indians or threatened by bandits. But as luck had it he escaped every time.

When it was at its most exciting Percy had to go to the toilet.

"Did you have to poo such a long time," I said when he came back. "Carry on."

He cleared his throat and read:

They shot me time and time again. But my good luck held and I came away in one piece. My horse was a Californian roan, the fastest in the stable. I jabbed my spurs in his flank and, crouched over the horse's neck, I headed for Sweetwater Bridge, twenty kilometres away.

"What a man," said Grandpa. "And to think that he was only fifteen."

"I'm only ten," said Percy.

Then he said that he had to go to bed, so he could manage the next day.

CHAPTER SIXTEEN

The impossible becomes possible, then impossible

The next morning Grandpa was brushing out the water urn with a steel brush. It squeaked so that everyone shivered and lost their appetite.

"Please Father," said Dad. "Can't that wait? I can't eat with that noise."

"Make hay while the sun shines," said Grandpa. "There's going to be a storm from the seventh heaven."

"That hardly seems possible," said Dad. "Look at the sky."

We all looked at the sky.

It was clear blue, with just two small puffy clouds. The wind was dry and warm.

"Don't talk rubbish," said Grandma.

"You'll see, you'll see," said Grandpa. "You'll be able to wash your hair soon."

Grandma loved to wash her hair in real rainwater, because it was so soft.

"Men can talk all they like but it's in the lap of the gods," said Grandma. "But if you're right, you'll be able to wash your feet. And that is truly necessary."

Just then Percy arrived with his hair all ruffled. He had no wounds, and he looked even happier than usual.

"A little porridge for you, Percy?" asked my mother.

"No thanks, no time," he said. "Come on Ulf." He pulled me up.

"Where are you off to?" Dad wondered.

"To a love match," said Percy.

He grabbed a crust of bread and put it in his pocket.

"Where are we going?" I asked.

"Can't tell you," he said. "But you're gonna be blown to bits. Boy oh boy!"

We jumped over the fresh cow pats in the paddock. Then we cut over a field of stumps and headed hard left into the woods.

We carried on running a bit more. Percy stopped and caught his breath. And then I was amazed. In the clearing ahead of us, tied to a tree, was a black horse, enjoying the fresh grass. Every now and then it took a step forwards, and swished its tail to keep the flies off.

Its mane shone as if it had been washed in rainwater.

"Black Demon," I whispered. "Is that really him?"

"Yes, isn't he beautiful?"

When Percy whistled, he looked up. And he didn't look the slightest bit angry. If it's possible for a horse to look loving, that's what Black Demon looked like when he saw Percy. But when he saw me he put his ears back.

"There, there," said Percy, and he calmed down straight away.

"Have you stolen him?" I asked.

"You can't own anything that's alive," said Percy. "It owns itself. So that means you can't steal it either. I've just taken him out."

"He looks angry with me," I said.

"He'll get used to you," said Percy. "We'll just have to go carefully to start with. When he sees that we're friends, there'll be nothing to worry about."

Percy talked quietly to Black Demon while we slowly moved forwards.

"This is Ulf Gottfrid Stark," he said. "He's the best guy there is. Once he caused a fire just so I could see what it was like when the fire engines came. Friends like that don't grow on trees. Come and say hello now."

We had stopped a bit away from Black Demon.

He looked at me, and then shook his head, as if he'd seen enough. He came forward and lay his heavy head on Percy's shoulder to be patted and to get the piece of bread. But before that he put his nose in my chest and gave me a friendly nudge, to show that he didn't have anything against me.

"There you are," said Percy.

"Is this really Black Demon, the angriest horse in Sweden?" I asked.

"Yep," said Percy. "Except he isn't so angry any more."

"What have you done?" I said.

"I've talked to him," said Percy.

"About what?" I said.

"About all sorts of things," he said. "But mostly about myself. I told him about how I grew up and what I think is good and bad in life. You have to talk about yourself so they know who you are. Then I showed him round. Is there any place you'd like to show him, Ulf?"

"Maybe the hill with the beacon," I said. "The view from there is nice."

"Then let's go," said Percy.

He put a bridle on Black Demon. Then off we went.

"Here it is!" I said.

"Crikey that's beautiful," said Percy. "You see that, Black Demon?"

Percy and the horse looked around with big eyes. From the beacon you can see so far it almost makes you dizzy. You can see at least three lighthouses. Some days you can see five.

"Those are called lighthouses," Percy told Black Demon. "And a couple of nudists live over there. There's not much to see, but still."

He turned to me.

"Which way is south-west?"

"Over that way," I said.

"That's the direction where we live, Black Demon," said Percy.

"You should come and visit us some time," I said.

Black Demon whinnied.

That's how we talked, Percy, Black Demon and I. The sky was still blue, but you could see black stripes on the horizon.

We had led Black Demon the whole way to the look out, even though Percy said it was easy to ride him now. He said he'd been riding the whole morning, and yesterday as well. But still it was best to let the horse get used to me for a while, before I got up on his back.

"What do you mean?" I said. "I can't ride."

"You have to," said Percy.

"Why should I do that?"

"For love," he said.

142

Then he reminded me about what Pia had said.

She had said it would be as impossible for her to fall in love with me as it would be for someone to ride Black Demon.

"It means that if anyone can ride Black Demon, then she can be in love with you."

"Yeah, bloody all right!" I said.

I didn't usually like swearing. But now Percy with his clear-as-glass logic had proved that Pia could be in love with me. I could have hugged him. Now I understood where Percy had been every morning. He'd been in Österman's stable and he'd got all his wounds teaching Black Demon to be nice. He was a saint. He was my blood brother for all time.

"Thanks," I said.

Then I wondered how he came to know so much about horses.

"I learned in Stockholm," he said.

He'd lived next door to a slaughterhouse – where old and sick horses were brought to be put down.

"I used to visit them in the paddock," said Percy. "They looked so sad. And I was quite sad myself at the time because I didn't have any friends there. But the old man who looked after the horses taught me to ride, because he said the old wrecks needed to have something else to think about other than death."

"Did they forget to be sad?" I asked.

"For a moment maybe. But now you should tell Black Demon the names of all the islands and lighthouses while I help you up on his back," said Percy. "Because soon Pia will be coming along the road."

We waited for her at the dance pavilion. Percy leaned against a film poster. And I – I almost couldn't believe it myself – sat on Black Demon's back behind some bushes, so that I couldn't be seen from the road. Percy led us there and spoke quietly in the horse's ear before he left us.

I patted Black Demon on the neck because I was feeling nervous.

"Please please stay calm now," I whispered. "Because the girl coming now is the girl I'm in love with. Everything depends on you."

"Hmmmm," said Black Demon, and cleared his throat as if he was about to say something.

But he didn't have time. Just then I saw through a gap in the bushes that Percy had gone out onto the road. And next moment Pia had stopped on her bicycle. She was wearing a light blue jersey.

"Hi," she said.

"Hi," said Percy. "What a beautiful jersey."

"Do you think so?" she said.

"Yes," he said. "Do you remember what you said the last time we met here, when Ulf was with us?"

"Of course I do," she said.

"You said it would be as impossible for you to go out with him as it would be to ride Black Demon. Remember?"

"Of course," she said.

Then Percy gave a low whistle and then a higher one – his special Black Demon whistle. And straight away Black Demon trotted out from behind the bushes and onto the road with me on his back. I squeezed tight with my knees and sat as straight as a stick. Pia rolled her eyes and looked like she was going to scream.

"Don't scream," I said. "It might make him angry again."

"Black Demon," she said. "Is that really Black Demon? That's not possible."

"Nothing is impossible," I said. "Now we can go out together."

I smiled. Maybe Black Demon smiled too. But Pia looked at me with serious eyes.

"Well," she said. "I'm sorry. But it still won't work."

"But we've proved it," I said.

"It was almost like a promise," said Percy.

"Yes, but it still wasn't what I meant," she said.

I looked at Percy. He didn't say anything. He just got up in front of me on Black Demon and took the reins. It was hopeless. I understood that now myself. We rode back to Österman's stable in silence. The sky got darker and darker. I struggled with myself so that I wouldn't turn around and look at Pia.

It was over.

It didn't do any good that we were greeted like heroes in the village because we had tamed Black Demon. Everyone wanted to pat us on the back. Österman tried to give us chewing tobacco. Grandpa took off his hat and bowed. His bald head was shining with pride.

"You are now seven thousand genius steps away from being idiots!" he said.

You can't get better praise than that.

But how can you feel joy when you can't have the girl you love?

That evening, the wind started to blow. It wailed from the black horizon, caught its breath, so the waves were blown away, and then it blew out as hard as it could. It pushed the tips of the waves in front of it towards the beach, bubbling and spitting out scum.

I stood on the jetty farthest out, soaked from the spray, and screamed into the sea all the swear words I had learned from Grandpa through the years.

"Why did you have to do this?" I shouted to the skies.

The answer thundered like a block of stone from the heavens.

CHAPTER SEVENTEEN

I decide God is not at all peaceful

The days that followed were heavy and wet. Grandpa spent his time in the workshop straightening out old nails. Grandma sat in her window. Mum kept the fire in the woodstove going. My brother built an aircraft carrier model out of plastic. Dad listened to the weather report.

"Quiet! They're doing East Svealand!" he called.

Just then, in the middle of the low front, Klaus knocked at the door. He looked a bit thinner than before.

"I'm back again," he said. "I heard down in the village that Pia turned you down."

"Does everybody know?" I sighed.

"I think so," he said. "I thought that you might as well have these."

He handed over a box in gift-wrapping. In it was his collection of dead beetles.

"Dad won't have them in the house," he said. "But they might make you feel better. We can play battles with them now."

We divided our armies on the floor in the back cabin. Klaus gathered up an air flotilla of dung beetles, ladybirds, and sloebugs. Percy put together a naval base of divers, water striders and boatmen, while General Stark arranged his ground troops: carrion beetles, burying beetles and a rhino beetle.

"What was it like eating bark then?" asked Percy.

"Not good," said Klaus. "But fried flies were worse. Is there anything left of that tiger cake?"

"It's all gone," I said. "But I can get you something else."

I got him half a sausage.

Then the war began. The dung beetles flew around dropping stone bombs. The fighter sloebugs decimated all my carrion beetles, so the burying beetles had to take care of them. And the rhino beetle was hit by a hand grenade that turned it into insect mash. After a while I didn't have a single insect remaining. The floor was a carpet of crushed bodies.

It was a gloomy sight. General Stark wasn't in form.

"What's the matter with you?" asked Klaus.

"You know what," I said.

So we tried playing some old games instead. We played pick-up sticks and Ludo, but I lost every time. I was thinking about other things.

"Have you lost your brain in a puddle, Ulf?" asked Klaus.

"Yes," I said.

"I have to go home for lunch again," he said. "Do you want to come down to the village?"

"No," I said.

I was shamed down there for ever and eternity. I would never be able to go down again. God had really mucked things up for me.

And I wasn't alone in this.

When Klaus had gone I looked for proof in the Bible about how God mucked things up for people. It wasn't difficult. The whole of the Old Testament was full of stories like that.

"Look at this one!" I said to Percy.

I showed him the picture of *The Pharaoh's army drowning in the Red Sea*, where a whole lot of soldiers and horses were drowned in huge waves. Then we looked at the pictures of the Flood, all the time the rain smattered down on our roof, rippling in the drain pipes and running down the windows.

"He's a tough guy, God is!" said Percy.

"Yes, he likes pouring water on his creation," I said.

After a while Dad came in and wanted a snooze after lunch.

So we went out and saved worms and snails from drowning. We put them in the wooden box where Grandpa kept his shoe polishing things. We took out the tins and brushes and filled the box with small creatures. Then we placed the box on the veranda to keep it high and dry.

ULF AND PERCY'S ARK, we wrote on the outside.

"They should say thank you," said Percy.

"Yeah, and they should write about us in the *First book of Snail*."

After dinner it began to thunder. It was dark inside, but Grandma didn't want to turn on the lights, because she was sure the electricity would attract the lightning.

"That's an old wive's tale," said Dad. "There is no evidence for it."

But we still weren't allowed to turn the lights on.

And Mum wasn't allowed to sing in the kitchen while she was baking either.

"But you don't think that I will attract the lightning," said my mother.

"You never know," said Grandma.

151

Mum giggled and hummed a song called *Rain, rain on me*.

Grandma had been afraid of thunder ever since she was little, when a bolt of lightning had curved in through their door, bounced like a fire-ball through the cottage, burned the cat's tail and gone twice around the kitchen table. Then it left again, as suddenly as it had arrived.

Now she sat in the sofa with her hands clenched and she looked older and more wrinkly than usual. And behind all the wrinkles, there was a terrified child with a glittering fire in her eyes. Dad sat close to her. He had laid his hand on her knee, so she wouldn't feel so alone. He explained everything about electricity – about electrons and lightning conductors.

"By the way, do you know who discovered the lightning conductor, Ulf?" he said.

"Benjamin Cricket," I said.

I said it to be funny, but nobody laughed.

"No, Benjamin Franklin," said Dad. "There is one on the roof of the school so Mother doesn't need to worry."

Dad thought that his mother would be calmed by science.

"Are you sure the kitchen door is closed, Kurt," she said.

"You have asked me that twice," he said. "There's

no danger. The thunder is a long, long way from here."

"But it's coming closer," I said. "That time I only managed to count to ten."

I was counting how long it took from the time you saw the lightning to when you heard the boom of thunder. That told you how many kilometres away the danger was, if you counted at a medium pace.

But now I was counting more slowly to scare Grandma.

My brother and I had always done that. But now he had grown out of thunder. He lay in his bed reading a comic by the light of his torch. But Percy and I kept watch at the window. We saw a flicker of light.

"You see that Grandma?" I called. "What lightning, eh!"

Then I counted really slowly so I only got to five.

"Now it's only five kilometres away!" I called.

I don't know why it was so much fun to scare Grandma. Maybe it was because she was always so calm otherwise. Normally she sat in her own world, like she was in a bubble of cigarette smoke. And today when I was sad it felt even better to frighten her.

"Soon it will be on top of us," I said.

And then there really was a powerful bolt of lightning. It made a Z of blinding light on the dark sky, as if Zorro had drawn it there with his sword. It didn't take long before the boom of thunder made the windows rattle.

Grandma put her hands over her eyes.

"Did you see that one!" I shouted. "Wow!"

We hadn't heard Grandpa come in from the workshop. He stood in the doorway. Rain dripped from the edge of his hat. And he looked angry.

"Are you frightening Grandma?" he shouted. "Stop it immediately!"

"You don't need to be afraid, Erika," he said to Grandma.

"God will look after me," she said.

Then I got really furious.

"God!" I shouted. "How can you believe God will look after anybody? He never does. And how is it possible to be called something so stupid as Gottfrid?"

Gottfrid means peace of God.

"Ah ha, so you think that's a stupid name?" said Grandpa.

"You should not insult God, Ulf," said Grandma.

"It is he who insults me," I said.

"Please Ulf," said Grandma. "You don't know what you're saying. God is love!"

"He's not love at all," I shouted. "And what do you know about love, Grandma? You can't even love Grandpa even though he's loved you all his life. That's been a big heavy rock for him. Why couldn't you love him back?"

"I don't know why," she said.

Then Grandpa punched the door frame.

"All of you be quiet!" he shouted. "None of you say another word, do you hear! I am going out to wash my feet. And when I come in again I don't want to hear a sound."

We heard him running warm water from the tap. Then he went out with the big copper bath, slamming the door behind him.

It was as if Grandpa took all the sound with him when he went.

It was as if the house and the wind and the storm all held their breath. We thought it was all over, that the clouds had turned and the sun was coming. Grandma got up, and was on her way to the mirror on the wall to comb her hair.

Then suddenly the room lit up as if someone had suddenly turned on a thousand lights at the same time. And then came the bang. It made the mirror on the wall slip sideways, the barometer squeak and the walls shake. Hissing blue sparks ran around the electrical cables in the ceiling. The black telephone in the hall rang and rang by itself.

"Don't answer it, boys," said Grandma. "It's the lightning."

"Oh my God," said Mum, putting her hands over her face even though they had dough on them.

A moment later Grandpa came into the room. He was white in the face. His trouser legs were rolled up and his feet left wet marks on the floor. The little bit of hair he still had stood straight up on his head. He hopped towards us, gasping for breath. I looked at his legs. You could see his veins as if someone had drawn them in ink on the outside of his skin.

"What happened?" asked Dad.

"That devil's lightning landed on my feet," said Grandpa.

Then Grandma got up. She went towards Grandpa with open arms. He stood still and saw her coming towards him. He had got hold of the door frame and clutched it so tightly his knuckles turned white.

He rocked backwards and forwards and looked at Grandma.

"Dear, dear man," she said.

Grandpa's eyes were completely red. Now he blinked.

"Do you love me, Erika?" he asked.

"Please Gottfrid," she said. "Don't talk now."

"Do you love me?" he repeated.

"No," she whispered as quietly as she could.

Then he lifted up his arms and sank them down again. He blinked again, as if he no longer recognised what he saw any more. Then he stumbled out into the rain.

"Father," said Dad.

I saw Grandpa's chubby figure through the window. He went towards the black stone in the strawberry patch. He rested his forehead against it. Then he put his arms around it. Then he gave an almighty yell and lifted it. For a moment he stood still, rocking, almost surprised at its terrible weight. Then he stumbled to the edge and shoved it over.

He stood and watched the stone roll down to the water.

"I got you in the end!" he yelled.

And then he fell.

"Oh my God," whispered Grandma.

We had to go to the school teacher to ask for help, because otherwise we never would've managed to carry Grandpa inside to the sofa. Dad shone Jan's torch into his eyes and listened to his heart. And then he asked Grandpa if he knew what his name was.

"Don't talk rubbish," he muttered.

"He's had a stroke," said Dad.

An hour later the doctor came and said the same thing. The doctor wanted Grandpa to be sent away in an aeroplane to the hospital. But then Grandpa grabbed hold of the sofa.

"You'll never get me away from here," he said. "Never. NEVER!"

"Dear Father," said my father.

Then Grandpa wrote on a piece of paper, because he couldn't speak any more: THERE'S NOTHING DEAR ABOUT ME. NEVER HAS BEEN.

"I can't have this on my conscience," said Dad.

"Then I'll have it on mine," said Grandma.

Before we went to bed that evening, I went into the back cabin by myself and looked up the Bible. I leafed through to page 483, where I thought I'd seen the lightning bolt that hit Grandpa's feet.

And there it was.

Elias allows fire to fall from heaven, the picture was called.

There was a white fork of lightning from the dark cloud at the top of the page, like a gigantic welding flame from outer space. It burned one of the old men at the bottom of the page – he was a heap of black ash.

That's what happened when you annoyed God.

That's what I'd done.

I leant my forehead against the page in the Bible,

just like I used to do on the floorboards in the boat when I got seasick.

"Dear God, don't take any notice of what I said. I was just very sad. The main thing is that Grandpa gets well. He's had enough bad things. You'd have to agree, wouldn't you?"

Then the telephone rang.

But it wasn't God. And it wasn't the lightning. It was Percy's mother who wanted to talk to him to say that they were very well and tell him how their travels had been and ask how things were with him.

"Things are good," I heard Percy say.

CHAPTER EIGHTEEN

Where has my hair gone, boys?

From that day on Grandma looked after Grandpa. No one else was allowed to look after him. She fried his chops for lunch and dinner and cut them into nice small pieces. She brushed his false teeth and carried out his bed pan. She aired the sheets, cut his toenails and dried him with a warm towel.

Every now and again Grandma sat in Grandpa's cabin to talk to him. He lay there with his blue eyes looking at the ceiling. Sometimes he smiled as if he could see something up there. I'd seen it myself, because Percy and I were also allowed in his room.

"What can you see, Grandpa?" I asked.

"The sky over the prairie," he said.

He wasn't himself. He didn't even have the energy to fart. And the curtain was pulled across all day because he couldn't tolerate the light.

"Go'natt to you boys," he said, in the morning and in the evening. "Would you like to read a paragraph or two, Percy?"

Percy didn't mind at all.

He would take down the old book about Buffalo Bill and read. And the strange thing was, the older Buffalo Bill came to be in the book and the more adventures he had, the better Grandpa became. He chuckled to himself, as if he suddenly remembered things he thought he had forgotten.

"That's right," he said. "Keep going."

And so Percy did.

It is possible that both Wild Bill and I drank more than we should have that afternoon. General Carr said to me: "Cody, there are a lot of antelopes around these parts. You could do a bit of hunting while we are here." I wasn't slow to take up the challenge. The hunt was a good one for me. I shot twenty or twenty-five antelopes a day and kept the whole camp in fresh meat.

"Yes, that's how it was, boys," muttered Grandpa. "Twenty-seven thundering antelopes, no more, no less. That's right, it was twenty-eight. I remember. Those were the days."

Then he farted for the first time in ages.

It was just a quiet creeper, but it was a fart at least.

"You'll be better soon," I said.

"I might not want to be, Ulf," he whispered. "But don't tell anyone."

"No," I said.

"One more thing," he said. "Ask Grandma if she still has the card with the writing on it. You know the one I mean?"

"Yes," I said.

"Then ask her if she will bring it with her next time."

I asked her straight away. Grandma was in the kitchen and washing up Grandpa's lunchtime plate, humming to herself.

"Grandpa wants to know if you still have the card from Buffalo Bill," I said. "Do you have it?"

Grandma turned so that the evening sun coloured her cheeks red.

"What does he want with that?" she said.

"I don't know," I said.

Percy and I had a lot to do now that Grandpa was in bed. He had a whistle on his bedside table and he blew it whenever he wanted to tell us what to do.

"Chop wood!"

So we did.

We did the weeding, we dug potatoes, fixed a drain

162

and collected rainwater from the water barrels so Grandma could wash her hair.

She did this twice a week now, to make Grandpa happy.

"How are you, Ulf?" said Percy one day when we were busy sooting the pot belly stove. "Have you stopped being sad about Pia?"

"I'm still sad," I said. "But I haven't had so much time to think about it."

"Shall we go down to the village and see if you can meet her?"

"I never will," I said.

"Maybe not," he said. "It's like eating spinach. You have to get used to it a little bit at a time."

"I s'pose so," I said.

Then we heard Grandpa's whistle. We rushed over and when we raced in he was sitting with two pillows behind his back looking at the clock. On the bedside table was the card from Buffalo Bill.

"Slow as a wet week, you slugs!" he said.

He seemed a lot better on the whole.

"What would you like, Grandpa?" I asked.

"Grandpa this, Grandpa that," he muttered. "I want to see what I look like, of course. Bring me a mirror. Make it snappy!"

We rushed off to get the hand mirror Grandpa had

carved from cherry wood for Grandma. We were back in less than a minute.

Grandpa was looking at the picture of the buffalo hunter on a horse.

"Were we fast?" Percy asked.

"Na-jah," said Grandpa. "Give me the mirror. Draw the curtains!"

When the sunshine poured in he had to blink, because his eyes weren't used to the light. It was like when you've been to a daytime movie and you come out into light from the darkness of the theatre.

He held up the mirror and looked at himself, closely and for a long time.

"What is it?" asked Percy. "Aren't you pleased?"

"Pleased and pleased," he said, his voice uncertain. "I'm not sure. I don't recognise myself. Do I really look like this?"

"What would you look like otherwise?" I said.

"I had thought my face would be longer and thinner," he said. "Lord help us, I look like a bloody dumpling up top! Where has my hair got to, boys? And my beard?"

"What hair?" I asked.

"All that long hair that was blowing in the wind," Grandpa said.

"It probably blew away," said Percy. "But your beard is growing. Feel how much stubble you've got already."

Percy stroked his hand over Grandpa's stubbly chin.

"That's true," said Grandpa. "I'll have to wait till it grows out again."

He gave the mirror back. Then he closed his eyes. He breathed calmly and quietly as if he was asleep. We were just about to pull the curtain across, when he opened his eyes.

"There you are," he said, as if we'd just popped up out of nowhere. "I was wondering if you'd be so kind as to pick me a bunch of nasturtiums. Also the biggest damned bunch of nettles you can lay your hands on, and a glass of sea water."

"What will you do with all those things?" I asked.

"I want to remember how things are," he said. "When I pushed away that damned stone it took a whole lot of other things along with it. Smells and tastes and memories and things."

"Memories of what?" asked Percy.

"Nothing for you to worry your small wrinkly brain with," he said. "Go on! And take a garden glove with you."

He waved us away.

"But come straight back," he said.

"Where are you off to?" called Dad from the deckchair outside.

He always looked up from his crossword now whenever we ran past.

"Just getting a glass of sea water for Grandpa," I said.

"Does he want sea water now as well?" Dad said. "Do you know what I found yesterday on the balcony?"

"No," I said.

"His shoe box. And do you know what he had put inside? Snails and worms!"

"We put them there," said Percy. "We were saving Creation."

"It's very nice that you are trying to protect him," he said. "But he still should be in the hospital."

Then he went back to his crossword and we carried on down to the beach and filled a glass from the fjord. Then we went back past the cellar door where the nettles grew and pulled off a good bunch. We carried on to the nasturtiums, picked some and took everything back to Grandpa.

"What are you going to do now, Grandpa?" I wondered.

"Smell the nasturtiums," he said.

He put the red-yellow flowers under his big nose and breathed deeply so the petals were sucked into his nostrils.

166

"That's what they smell like," he said. "Not bad."

Then he took the glass of sea water. He sniffed it as well and then he took a big gulp, gurgled, and swallowed. He made a face and spat and spat.

"Bah! Yuk!" he snorted. "That's exactly it! I'll be damned, it tastes awful."

He asked us to rinse out his false teeth so he could get rid of the taste. Then he put on the gardening glove, took hold of the stinging nettle and put it directly onto his arm. He winced as if he had been prodded with a red-hot poker.

"Aaaaooh," he yelled. "Just as I thought. It hurts like fire."

"I know," I said. "Shall I get the vinegar?"

"If you don't mind," said Grandpa.

This time it was me who got to bathe Grandpa's nettle rash.

"How is it?" he said while I was doing it. "Is there still pain in your heart?"

"Yes," I said.

"Do you know what," he said. "You can't help it if you don't love another person. You can't decide that yourself. But you should try not to love someone who can't love you back."

"I know that all right," I said. "But you can't decide that for yourself either."

"No, that's true," said Grandpa.

Then he settled himself with the nasturtiums on the pillow, waiting for his beard to grow. When we were sneaking away for a swim he called out,

"Say hello to General Carr, boys!"

CHAPTER *NINETEEN*

I think about boiled cod's eyes

A couple of days later we sat on the garden seat peeling potatoes. We'd dug up the brown clumps from the potato patch ourselves. We had them in a bucket of sea water so the mud would wash off. Peeling them was a slow job, because I wasn't used to it.

We used to always boil the potatoes with their skins on. But ever since Grandpa got lightning in his feet, he wanted them peeled.

The pot slowly filled with clean, white potatoes.

"This one looks like General de Gaulle," I said.

"And this one is like Lex Luthor," said Percy about one that was round and ugly.

One a Frenchman, the other Superman's worst enemy.

This was how we kept happy. After a while, Grandpa came. He had been up the hill raising the flag.

"Don't work yourselves to the bone, boys," he said.

"Work is fun," said Percy.

"I can think of one or two other things that are more fun," he said.

He wasn't himself. He was more cheerful, and happier than usual.

He had started to get around again. But he walked with his back straighter than before. He was always properly dressed in hat and waistcoat. But he didn't want to wear his glasses, so sometimes he got lost. But he didn't care.

"If you don't get lost, you'll never find anything new," he said.

One day he ended up at the shoemaker. He took the opportunity to order himself a new pair of leather boots with a half-high heel and seams on the leg – a sort that no one had ever seen in the village before. He even paid cash in advance without a grumble.

These days he also popped in a few American phrases now and then when he was speaking.

"Gottfrid, come in!" called Grandma, because she was worried about him.

"Love is calling," said Grandpa, winking at us. "See you later, boys!"

Then he rubbed his fingers over his chin to see if his beard was growing. It was. It had grown quite a lot and was completely white.

"Soon," he muttered. "Very soon." Then he went inside.

When Grandpa had gone Percy and I kept on peeling potatoes in silence. I thought about how nice Grandma had been to Grandpa recently. And then I started to think about Pia. She should have been like that too, I thought.

I threw a potato into the bucket of water so it splashed.

"What is it, Ulf?" asked Percy.

"I'll never be free," I said. "I was thinking about Pia. I thought I'd forgotten her. But I never will."

"What were you thinking?"

"About how she smells," I said. "And about how she sniffs when she has a cold. And how she sits on the seat when she is biking somewhere."

"Do you like thinking about those things?" asked Percy.

"Of course I do!"

"That's the trouble," said Percy. "That's the thing you have to stop."

"Thanks," I said. "And how will that happen?"

"Close your eyes and think of her, you'll see!" he said.

So I did. At first I saw nothing. But then I could see Pia leaning over me, like that time an eternity ago when I tried to get her pike and fell in and hurt my

171

eyebrow. I saw her encouraging eyes on mine and her worried expression. Soon I would feel the pink bathing towel with her smell on it over my nose. I knew that.

"Can you see her in front of you now?" said Percy in a low voice.

"Yes," I whispered.

It was like pure magic.

And just at that moment Percy heaved the bucket of dirty sea water, old peel, de Gaulle, potato Luthor and two kilos of hard lumps over my worried skull.

"What on earth do you think you're doing!" I shrieked.

"It's for your own good," he said.

"You're not right in the head!" I spat.

Then he explained that this was the only way for me to get over my love for Pia. I had to do something really horrible every time I thought about her. Then I would feel sick as soon as I saw her.

"I'll help you," he said.

"Nice of you," I said, feeling the filthy water running down my back.

Then we went down to the jetty and filled the bucket with sea water, finished the potatoes and carried them in to Mum.

"Dinner will be in an hour," she said.

"Then I'll pop down to Black Demon to say hello,"

Percy said. "So he doesn't think I've forgotten him. Are you coming?"

"Nup,' I said. "I've got to wash my hair."

But when I had rinsed out the dirt and put on a clean shirt, I sneaked down to the peninsula with the crayons I'd been given for my birthday.

I saw a pike head in a crevice. It was sneering at me with sharp teeth and empty eyeball sockets. I remembered that pike. It was the one Pia was cleaning when we'd arrived.

"Pia," I said, and then I hit myself on the cheek to get rid of love.

Then I went in to the shelter by the jetty. I saw what was written on one of the walls:

IF YOUR HEART SHOULD EVER BREAK
FIX IT UP WITH SELLOTAPE

I had written that myself. Now I took out the red crayon and wrote in even bigger letters:

IT'S ALL RUBBISH!

Then I closed the door and sat in the dark so that no one would see the tears.

In the following days Percy did his best to cure me of love.

To start with we lay behind a stone up on the hill by the beacon. We had Grandpa's binoculars with us. We were waiting for Pia to come past on her bicycle on her way to the shop.

"There! Here she comes," said Percy. "Look now. And remember what you have to do."

He passed me the binoculars. I put them to my eyes with shaking hands. And even though I did what he said and turned the binoculars back-to-front so that she just looked like a little insect a long, long way away, it still hurt inside me.

"What are you thinking about?" asked Percy.

"Pia," I said.

"Get a grip on yourself," he said. "You have to concentrate. Well?"

"Liver," I said. "Liver and burnt potatoes."

"And more?" he said.

"Pork cubes in white sauce," I said.

And suddenly I felt better. I couldn't see her sweet face any longer in my inner vision. I saw a white, sticky mess with wobbly fatty bits in it and I felt slightly sick. I even managed to turn the binoculars the right way round again when she'd finished shopping and was on her way back.

"How does it feel?" Percy asked.

"Not so good," I said. "But I'm on the way to feeling better."

He patted me on the shoulder, pleased.

174

"Bravo Ulf," he said. "Tomorrow we can creep up a bit closer. And you can think of something even worse."

But when we came home Percy's father had rung. He and his mother had come back from their camping holiday. They'd had a good time, even though it rained a lot. Now they wanted their son back. And his father had asked whether Percy had learned to swim twenty metres yet.

"Damn," said Percy.

"It will be fun to see them," said Mum.

"Yeah, of course it will," said Percy.

"There's not such a hurry," said Grandpa.

"What do you say, Percy?" asked Dad. "Won't it be nice to go home?"

"Yes," said Percy and he looked at me. "But I need four more days."

They were terrible days.

He had to learn to swim those twenty metres without putting his feet on the bottom. And I had a lot to learn before I was over Pia.

In the mornings I swam with Percy down by our jetty. And in the afternoons we spied on Pia so that I could practise thinking of horrible things.

I thought about when I broke a window at home and Dad was angry. And when I fell off the swing and hit the back of my head, so that the white jersey Mum had knitted got sticky with blood and I had to get stitches. And when I was visiting a friend and ate herring to be polite, even though I was allergic and I vomited over his mother's dress.

There were a lot of horrible things for me to think about.

Now we were standing behind a bush at the pavilion, waiting for Pia on her bicycle. I saw her summer-brown feet pedalling flat out, her shirt fluttering.

I was thinking about the vomit from my childhood and I held a cold wet toad against my stomach under my jersey.

It might help, Percy had said. And it did.

I was about to vomit once more.

"Good," he said. "Tomorrow you'll meet Pia for a very short time."

"It'll be hard," I said.

"It's your last chance," he said.

We went down to the village after lunch the next day. At first we looked for her outside her house, but she wasn't there. We found her by the old abandoned lighthouse. There was Ulf E, Klaus, Birgitta, Leif and Kicki as well. They were all swimming. They had lit a fire by the water even though it was forbidden.

Pia sat on a rock by the fire, wrapped in her towel. We stood behind an alder tree.

"Do it now," whispered Percy.

"Aw, let's just forget about it," I said.

"No," he said. "You have to talk to her. And the whole time you have to think about you know what."

"Yes," I said.

I went up to her. Percy followed to make sure I didn't cheat. Klaus, Leif and the others didn't say anything.

"Hello," I said.

"Hello," said Pia, without even looking up. "What do you want?"

"Just to say hello," I said.

I looked at her and felt my stomach tighten, so that I had to swallow.

"Why are you staring like that?" she said. "And why are you pulling those faces? What are you thinking about?"

"Boiled cod's eyes," I said.

Klaus smiled. But I had to swallow. That was the worst thing I knew; when Grandma picked out the eyes from the boiled cod, popped them in her mouth and chewed. I usually looked away. But now I imagined how those white small balls with black pupils were being mashed to bits by her teeth.

"How nice," said Pia. "And you Percy? What are you thinking about?"

"About how I'm going home soon," he said. "But it was nice to meet you."

"Yes," she said.

After that we all went up to the house together. But before we left Klaus made the V-sign to me with his fingers. That meant victory. I had won. The swallows were dive-bombing high in the sky. A crested peewit hopped over the path. And Percy put his arm around me.

"You did very well," he said. "How does that feel now?"

"I still feel sick," I said.

"Then you're probably over the worst," he said.

CHAPTER TWENTY

Grandpa shaves and becomes like new

The next day, Grandpa came out with a basin of warm water that he placed on a concrete shelf outside the cottage. He grinned broadly at the squirrels and the crows. His braces were hanging down by his sides, he'd pushed his hat back and he was only wearing a singlet on his upper body. He had his new leather boots on and he'd laid his checked shirt on the ground.

"You came just at the right time," he said.

"Why's that?" we asked.

"My lips are sealed," he drawled.

There was a patch of grass above the shelf where wild strawberries, poppies and nasturtiums grew. He'd stuck Grandma's mirror into the ground, so that it met the sun and was shooting out bolts of light. Beside it he had put the photo of Buffalo Bill wearing his leather jacket with the fringes and a wide-brimmed cowboy hat.

"Are you going to shave, Grandpa?" I asked.

"The prairies are calling," he said.

"What?" said Percy.

"I do what I have to do," he said.

Grandpa got the shaving cream ready in a coffee cup. A gull flew down and sat on the chimney to watch. Grandpa opened his shaving knife and drew it back and forth along a leather belt to sharpen it. He hummed a tune I'd never heard before. After a while, Grandma came outside and stopped on the steps.

"I was just going to say that..." she said.

She was probably going to say that lunch was soon ready. But she fell into silence. The sun reflected from the shaving knife into her eyes. She was blinded. And so she stayed standing, and watched while Grandpa soaped his cheeks and throat.

"Do you want something?" asked Percy.

But she just put her finger to her lips.

And Grandpa didn't say anything either, because he didn't want to risk cutting his throat, where his skin was wrinkly and hard to shave. But he winked at her in the mirror. He drew the knife over his cheeks and then rinsed off the white scum in the basin.

He simply shaved himself, and there was nothing special about that.

Still it was as if we were witnessing something of the

sort you could write about in the Bible, or in the book about Buffalo Bill.

In the end all Grandpa had left was a moustache and a tuft of hair on his chin. He took Grandma's nail scissors and shaped it, so it became a little pointed beard, just like Buffalo Bill had in the photo.

He put on his shirt.

He sat his hat firmly on his head.

Then he turned around to Grandma.

"Well, what do you think?" he said.

For a moment a shadow of worry passed over his face. But Grandma dried her hands on her apron and smiled.

"Dear Gottfrid," she said.

"Just call me Buffalo Bill," he said. "When is lunch ready?"

"Lunch? Of course, lunch," she said, blushing.

"I love you, sweetheart," he said.

But before he went in he turned to us. He took a piece of paper from his pocket.

"Psst. Give this to the school teacher," he whispered.

Grandma had set the big oak table with the best plates and a white tablecloth. And she had brought in wild flowers, briar roses, and nasturtiums, and put them in glass jars all around the room.

181

It was pork chops. Of course that's what Grandpa ate every day. But it was also what he liked best.

"I'm sorry, but the sauce went lumpy," she said.

"Don't worry," he said, even though he hated lumps.

He helped himself to potatoes and covered them in sauce. There were also carrots and peas in a deep dish for those who wanted them. Grandpa didn't.

But he did want a schnapps.

Grandma had placed a little glass of schnapps at his and Dad's places.

"Chingaling, junior!" said Grandpa, raising his glass.

"I'm not sure you should be drinking," said Dad.

"A little schnapps can't hurt," said Grandma.

They raised their glasses and drank. Then it was time to eat, although Grandma didn't eat much, because she found it hard to chew meat. She just ate boiled carrots and looked at Grandpa. I thought she looked like the big Peace rose she had cut and placed in a vase on the table. It was pink and white – she had white hair and pink cheeks.

"Does it taste good?" she asked.

"Swell," said Grandpa.

He looked happy, but he didn't say much. Then he suddenly stood up.

"Hang on a minute," he said. "There's something I've forgotten!"

He went over to the window and opened it. He took his whistle and blew a loud, shrill signal.

Then we heard a cough and the air was filled with the most beautiful piano music you could imagine. It sounded like the music from one of those cowboy films that Percy and I had seen by the hundreds. One of those ones where the man sits in a saloon in his round bowler hat and rolled-up sleeves, with a glass on the piano, playing something cheerful and sad, the moment before everyone pulls out their guns and starts shooting each other.

"I asked the school teacher to play a song for the prairie's most beautiful rose," said Grandpa. "Play it as long and as loud as you can, I wrote."

Grandma wiped her eyes with her napkin. Because it really was a fine tune and the school teacher only coughed a couple of times during the whole piece. But Dad pushed away his plate, even though it still had food left on it.

"Shouldn't we ring for the doctor just in case," he said.

"No, we shouldn't," said Grandma.

And when Grandpa gave her a kiss after dinner, she didn't pull away. Because it was the strangest thing, that even though she couldn't love Grandpa, she seemed to love this wobbly Buffalo Bill in a grey felt hat, and cowboy boots.

"Would you like to hear the final chapter of the book tonight?" asked Percy. "It's my last night."

"Thank you," said Grandpa. "But it won't be necessary. You're most welcome to read it yourselves. To be perfectly honest, boys, I've added in bits here and there. You have to if a book is going to sell well. And one more thing: don't wake me tomorrow morning. Because tonight I might get a little bit lost. And then I'll want to have a rest. But in the afternoon there'll be shooting, that's for sure."

We went down to the jetty that evening and had a swim, because we understood that we were in the way. A couple of bearded grebes swam with us without causing any trouble. But even though we kept on till the ships going past in the fjord had turned on their lights, Percy only managed to swim fifteen metres without putting his feet down.

We had painted clear black lines for every metre – and a red one at twenty – on a long rope across the bay, so I could see how far he'd got.

"Thirteen and a half," I said. "You're getting worse and worse."

"Not likely!" he said.

He was red in the face.

He spat out water and puffed.

"Just one more time," he said.

"Nope, we have to go up now," I said. "You're just getting tired. And besides, it's too dark to see the line."

"It's never going to work," he said, and he got up onto the jetty, took off his bathing suit and slapped it down with a splatter.

"Yes it will," I said. "You just have to practise a bit more."

"And when will I do that?" he snorted. "I'm leaving tomorrow afternoon."

We went up to the house with heavy steps.

Mum gave us a thermos of hot chocolate, a plate of cheese sandwiches and an apple each.

"Take this with you," she said. "You'd better go straight to bed."

And that's what we did.

We lay down in the ladies' salon, because ever since Grandpa had got his feet shot down by lightning, Grandma didn't want us sleeping in the hut. Grandpa said that we had better sleep in the house or he'd dump the hut in the sea with his own hands.

Jan had moved his mattress out into the hall, so we could be in peace.

Percy looked up at the ceiling, pensive.

185

"It's the only thing missing," he sighed. "Learning to swim those last darned metres."

"You'll be able to," I said.

"You're just saying that to cheer me up," he said.

"Yes," I said. "But I can't work it out. You're doing everything right."

"I know," he said. "Maybe I should do more dry swimming."

"No," I said. "It's better that you rest so you're fresh for tomorrow. I'll read *Buffalo Bill* for you."

I read how Buffalo Bill competed with his horse Big Bull and how he hunted herds of buffalo over the prairie and was chased by Indians. I read until Percy went to sleep.

I saw him making swimming movements in his sleep.

And after a while, I went to sleep myself.

But Buffalo Bill continued to ride his white horse through my dreams. In the distance, the old prairie wagons squeaked. The hooves of the herds of buffalo roared like thunder. And farther away, I could hear the prairie dogs howling at the moon.

Then I thought I could hear Grandma laughing quietly to herself.

CHAPTER TWENTY-ONE

Percy runs out of puff

The next day when Percy and I climbed into Grandpa's cabin, he wasn't there. He'd got lost, just like he said. On the bedside table there were just his false teeth smiling to themselves.

"Imagine if he's fallen into the sea," I said. "We'd better tell Grandma."

"She'll go crazy," said Percy.

But she didn't, because he had ended up getting lost in her room. He was lying beside her on the sofa with the carved lion's heads on the armrests. He was leaning his head against her shoulder, sleeping. He had dribbled a little bit on her nightdress. He looked very pleased. Grandma did too. When we peeped in through the gap in the door she opened her eyes a little bit and waved carefully with her hand. We understood we should go away.

We collected some empty cans and put them on the edge of the veranda outside Mum and Dad's window. Then we threw stones at them. PLONG and BONK, they said. It woke Mum.

"What are you up to?" she called.

"Won't breakfast be soon?" I called back.

So she got up and made a plate of scones – she'd found a recipe for them in an English magazine. She baked them for Percy, because he was going home on the boat that day. Dad ate most of them. He ate eight scones with butter and jam.

"These buns are really good," he said. "You have the last one, Percy."

"No thank you," said Percy. "Then I might get cramp and die."

"It's not going to be that bad," said my father.

"Yes it is, because we're going swimming."

We were already on our way to get our towels and our bathing suits from the clothes line.

"What would you like for lunch then, Percy?" asked Mum. "Today you can have whatever you like."

Mum raised her teaspoon. She looked like a house-wife fairy with a wand in her hand! If it had been me, I would have asked for two cheese sandwiches, rump steak with potatoes and gravy and chocolate éclairs with cream.

But Percy had other things on his mind.

"It doesn't matter," he said. "Pork chops. Buffalo Bill likes them."

We ran the whole way down to the jetty, firstly because we were so anxious to get to the water, and secondly, because when we had got up speed, we couldn't stop.

We ran right out onto the jetty.

Percy was first. We'd changed into our bathing suits at the house.

"First in is Johnny Weissmuller!" he yelled and then jumped.

Johnny Weissmuller was the guy who had played Tarzan in the Tarzan movies. He'd also been world swimming champion.

"AIAIAIAIAAH!" shouted Percy in mid-air.

He sounded like Tarzan, son of the apes.

"Second in is General Patton!" I shouted and jumped in after him.

General Patton did a belly flop. He was an American general in the Second World War. He was the toughest of everybody in the whole war. Now he bent down and took a handful of mud from the bottom of the bay, pressed the water out of it and shaped it into an egg-shaped hand grenade. It hit Johnny Weissmuller right in the skull.

This was the beginning of the Second Mud War.

Tarzan-Johnny was helped by animals. A platoon of hippopotamuses kicked up muddy water into the face of General Patton.

He responded by letting loose a volley of squelchy mud balls, so that Tarzan lost his footing and swallowed cold soup.

"That's because Pia fell in love with you," said Patton.

"Oh hell," coughed Tarzan.

He counter-attacked with the hippopotamuses. He placed them with their bottoms facing the enemy lines. With angry whirling tails they spread their dung over the entire seventh army. I was just going to take aid from the 91st Karlsson, when Klaus turned up, because it was Percy's last day.

"What are you doing?" he asked.

Johnny Weismuller became Percy again.

"We are just jumping around to digest our food," he said. "I'm going to swim twenty metres. It's now or never."

"Good luck," said Klaus.

Percy stood by the first line on our measuring rope. He rinsed the mud from his face, because he wanted to look good when he beat his record.

"Count to three, Ulf," he said, taking a deep breath.

"One – two – three," I said.

He started off well. For the first nine metres he glided forwards as quickly and easily as anything. Klaus even started to whistle the national anthem, he was so sure that Percy would do it.

But after twelve metres it was as if he'd lost all his energy. Still he carried on another five metres out of sheer will, before his head went down.

"Did you see that! I think he might have folded!" said Klaus, pretending to be a radio commentator.

"Shut up," I said.

Because I didn't want Percy to hear him.

Percy came up again. He only managed to get himself up onto the jetty by the skin of his teeth. I had to help him. He sat there puffing and hanging his head, his legs dangling.

"Seventeen metres," I said quietly. "A bit more than seventeen metres."

"Sod," he said.

"But you were doing very good strokes," said Klaus. "Among the best I've seen."

"Yes, they were," I said.

"What does that matter?" said Percy. "We're not having a competition for style."

"Next time will be the one," I said.

"There won't be a next time," said Percy.

"Why not?" I asked.

"Because I've run out of puff," he said. "I can't swim any further than that. It felt like I was going to burst. I saw a whole lot of black dots in front of my eyes. How can anyone swim across the English Channel. It's really long!"

"Thirty-three point eight kilometres," said Klaus. "As the crow flies. But because of the tides it can get up to more than fifty."

He was like a talking encyclopaedia.

"They cover themselves in grease," I said. "Shall we do that? We can use butter."

"No," said Percy. "I can't do it."

He lay on his back on the jetty, looking up at the grey sky. And the sun looked back through the clouds. It looked like a boiled cod eye without a pupil. I said so to Percy. He usually appreciated my similes. But not this time.

"Mmm," was all he said. He was probably thinking about his father.

Klaus and I lay beside him on the bridge, for company.

I closed my eyes and listened to Percy's sighing breaths and suddenly I realised what he was doing wrong.

"Into the water again," I said, giving him a shove.

"No," he said.

"You'll be able to do it this time," I said. "I know what you were forgetting to do before."

"What's that?" said Percy, showing a glimmer of interest.

I made a little pause to make the whole thing more exciting.

"To breathe," I said.

"Did I?" said Percy.

"Yes, you did actually," said Klaus.

"How could I forget that?" he said.

"I don't know," I said. "But you ran out of oxygen. Hop in."

So he did. I said that he should breathe in when he pulled his arms towards his body and breathe out when he stretched them out again. Everything would work itself out. He took a couple of swimming strokes to test it out. Then without waiting he started to swim the length of the rope. Every now and again he got water in his mouth and had to spit it out again. Otherwise it all went perfectly. It was no trouble at all for him to get to the red line.

"Now!" I called from the jetty when he reached it.

But he turned around and swam back again at top speed.

"Did you see, did you see?" he shouted, when he got to the jetty. "Now Dad will be happy. I did it! I swam twenty metres!"

"No," I said.

"What do you mean, you idiot!" he shrieked. "I did too!"

"No, you swam forty metres," I said. "Because you swam back again as well."

Then he slapped his chest. He had beaten the sea. He had beaten everything that had anything to do with water: streams, creeks, rivers, oceans and taps. Now he was Tarzan again, so happy he didn't know what to do with himself.

"AIAIAIAIAI AAH!" he shouted so that it echoed.

Then he heaved himself up onto the jetty and threw me into the water.

"What shall we do now?" said Klaus.

"Now we'll go and dig up carrots," he said.

CHAPTER TWENTY-TWO

Buffalo Bill shoots bull's-eyes every time

"What will we do with the carrots?" I asked.

"Shh. Don't be an idiot," whispered Klaus.

And then I understood that we were doing something dangerous, because we were digging them in Ericsson's garden, and he was known for being strict. As well as that his wife kept constant watch from the window. We dug up the six biggest carrots with our hands and rinsed them at the pump.

Percy put them up his jersey.

"Shall we ring the doorbell now?" whispered Klaus.

"What for?" said Percy.

"To make it exciting," I said. "Then we run."

Percy didn't have anything against that. We crept up the outside steps and pushed the doorbell. We held it in as long as we dared. Then we ran like small lunatics. We ran out through the gate, past the post-

195

box and Pia's house and then we swung off towards Österman's.

We were laughing the whole time.

Outside Österman's house Percy stopped and breathed out.

"Why have you stopped?" I asked.

"You should never be out of breath when you talk to a horse," said Percy.

He was going to visit Black Demon. He wanted to say goodbye to him, and to tell him about how far he'd swum.

Black Demon was now kept in a paddock outside the stable. As soon as he saw Percy he neighed softly and came up to the fence and nudged his soft nose to Percy's ear.

"Good day, dear horse," said Percy, popping a big carrot in Black Demon's mouth. "These come from Ericsson's garden, so they are of the best quality. Today, you know, is both a happy and a sad day. Happy because I learned to swim forty metres. And sad because I'm going home on the afternoon boat. So now I can't come here and say hello like I did before. But I will think of you every day around about three o'clock. I'll never forget you. And you'll never forget me either."

We stood there till the carrots ran out.

Then we left. Percy and I wanted to go home to Grandpa. And Klaus was going to help his father change the oil in their boat's motor.

"I'll come down later," he said.

When we got to the house Grandpa was already up. He came out of the woodshed as we coming up the path. He had sour milk with ginger in his moustache. The felt hat was on his head and the leather boots creaked when he walked, because they were so new. He smiled at us like a hero full of secrets.

And he had the cabin-rifle with him.

"So there you are, boys!" he said. "Best we get going straight away if anything is to be shot."

We went a little bit towards the school house, just a couple of hundred metres. Then Grandpa wobbled so much we had to catch hold of him.

"It's these stupid boots," he said. "They're not worn in yet."

Then I said that I could get him a stool so he could stop and rest whenever he wanted to.

"That's a good idea Ulf," he said. "But don't say a word to Grandma."

I ran back and stole the white stool from beneath the telephone in the hall. And while I was at it, I took the blanket from my bed, so that Grandpa wouldn't get cold legs while he was sitting.

When I was just about to sneak out, Grandma took me by the shoulder.

"You're going out with Grandpa, you and Percy, aren't you?" she said.

"Yes," I said, because I could see in her eyes that it wouldn't do to lie.

"I knew it, when he went and hid himself in the woodshed," she said.

I thought she would forbid it. But she didn't. She just said that we should be careful with him. Because he wasn't so steady on his legs, she said. And if you fell over at his age your legs could break.

"Don't be away too long because lunch will be ready soon," she added. "And don't say anything to Grandpa about what I said to you."

"No," I said.

She gave me a kiss on the forehead before I set off after Percy and Grandpa. They hadn't got very far. We went slowly up the hill to where the beacon was. Grandpa sat down quite often when he wanted to show us a cone or when he heard a bird he didn't recognise, or if he wanted to look more closely at the ants on the ground, to see where they were going.

"They work hard, those small devils," he said.

In the end Grandpa decided it was far enough. He sat down on the stool on a bit of grass, almost at the top of the hill, and I spread the blanket over his bad knee. So he sat there and looked at the fjord and the boats, till the white grey sky became a circus tent.

"Soon," he whispered.

"What's that?" I asked.

"Everything," he said.

And after a while he said: "Ladies and gentlemen." He took off his hat and bowed in every direction.

And suddenly it was as if the legs on the white stool had grown, as if it grew a neck with a dancing mane and a tossing head and it became the proud steed, Big Bull. Grandpa sat with his back straight, looking around at all the bushes, stones and trees that were swaying in the wind. And then I understood what he was seeing: Indians with swaying feathers, shooting cowboys, soldiers, stagecoaches travelling the prairie, and buffalos steaming forward with their heads down. It was the Wild West circus I had read about at the end of his book.

"And now," said Grandpa, and he swung his hat.

He dug out a bundle from his pocket. It was his handkerchief. It was full of shiny copper coins.

"Throw," Grandpa said. "Throw them as high as you can!"

So we did. We threw up all the coins in the air, one by one, and Grandpa sat on the stool and shot them. He lifted his rifle to his shoulder and pulled the trigger. And the strange thing was, that even though he saw so badly, he hit bull's-eyes almost every time.

"Next!" he called.

So we would throw up a new one.

We kept going till the show was over, as suddenly as it began. Grandpa lowered the rifle and bowed one last time. All around us were the shot-down coins, shining like small suns.

"We'll go home now, boys," he said. "The pork chops are probably ready."

They were.

It took quite a long time for us to get back. Grandpa sat down to rest every five minutes. Then we were home. He said to me to creep in from the back and to hide the rifle in the wardrobe. He threw his hat into his cabin, pulled off his boots and assumed an innocent look. When Grandma asked where we had been he said that he'd just been showing Percy nature's small miracles.

"Do you know what's the best thing about being away?" said Grandpa when we were sitting at the table and he was trying to get rid of a bit of meat that had got stuck between his teeth.

"No, what could that be?" said Mum.

"It's being able to come home," he said. "It's taking off your boots and just being yourself and forgetting about the audience."

"Do you think so too, Percy?" said Dad.

"I don't know," he said. "I haven't come home yet."

"No, that makes sense," said Dad.

But Grandpa laughed.

"You're not silly," he said.

And when lunch was finished, he went and got the silver dollar from his desk drawer. He came in just when Percy was packing the last thing in his bag. It was his bathing suit. It was still wet.

"Here," said Grandpa, holding out the shiny coin. "Just keep it. I don't need it any more."

Then Percy gave him a hug.

"It was so cool to meet you," he said.

Then we went down to the jetty.

The others were already standing there waiting to say goodbye: Klaus, Benke, Ulf E, Leif with his little sister on his shoulders, Birgitta, Marianne, Kicki. And then Pia.

"Maybe we will meet again sometime," Pia said to him when the boat had arrived.

"You never know," said Percy.

He waved to everyone before he went on board. But we didn't say anything, him and me. We didn't need to, because we knew we would see each other again soon.

Then the boat glided away. Klaus stood on my right side, and Pia was on the left.

"He was very nice," she said.

"Yes," I said.

After a while she lifted her hand halfway in my direction.

"Goodbye then," she said.

"Goodbye," I said. "Probably I can start talking to you again soon."

Then it was just Klaus and me on the jetty.

And farther down the beach, by a crushed black stone, Grandpa stood in his felt hat and his new leather boots and shot a salute when the boat went past. He shot straight up to the pale sun, as if it was a shiny silver dollar.

But it didn't fall down.